✦ ✧ ✦

Croning Tales

by Elayne Clift

Telling It Like It Is:
Reflections of a Not So Radical Feminist

But Do They Have Field Experience!

The Road to Radicalism:
Further Reflections of a Frustrated Feminist

Demons Dancing in My Head:
Collected Poems, 1985–1995

Croning Tales

✦ ✧ ✦

Croning Tales

Elayne Clift

OGN Publications

ISBN 0-9634827-3-4

"Benchmarks" first appeared in *Unknowns,* Spring, 1989.
"Standing Up to Eugene" was awarded First Place in the 1990 Dorothy Daniels Honorary Writing Award Competition of the National League of American Pen Women, Simi Valley Branch.
"Flashbacks" first appeared in *What's a Nice Girl Like You Doing in a Relationship Like This?,* Crossing Press, 1992.
"Rosie's Tape" first appeared in *Mediphors,* 1993.
"Seaplane" first appeared in *Journeys,* 1993.
"Helga's Day" first appeared in *Chips Off the Writer's Block,* 1993.
"The Talking Vase" first appeared in *Paradise,* Florida Literary Association, 1994.
"A Kind of Day" first appeared in *Pudding Magazine,* 1994.
"The Incident" first appeared in *Mature Years,* 1995.

———————

I am indebted to Kristin Cooney and Bethanne Licata for their editorial and production support, and to Jenna Dixon, Bookbuilder, for once again guiding me home. I also wish to thank Lindy Gifford for her wonderful cover design.

My gratitude also to Alison Tinsley, and the other women of my writer's group, for unconditional encouragement, sound critical analyses, and a great time.

And with love to my family, especially AJC, for so patiently nurturing the muse.

For the Crones,

and for
Alberta, Elizabeth, and especially Esther,
with deep gratitude for
the gift of your lives, your spirits, and your friendship

✦ ✧ ✦

Contents

✦ ✧ ✦

Preface

It is quite possible that the title of this collection will be misunderstood by many, an enigma to others. So perhaps it is best to explain.

Most people think of Crones as haggard, old, witchlike women (in the worst sense of that image) who have nothing to offer but evil spirits. Nothing could be farther from the truth. In pre-Christian, pre-patriarchal times, postmenopausal women were revered for their intellectual and spiritual gifts, and their counsel was sought by others because they were so wise. Healers and leaders, they were called upon at every occasion from birth to death, where they exercised the power of the ancient tribal matriarch.

I learned this from a little brochure I came across put out by The Feminist Institute Clearinghouse just as I was creeping up to my 50th birthday and wondering how I would mark my passage into the second half. Excited by what I had just read, I determined to have a Croning Celebration, sharing with special friends — women I had known through all the phases of my life — my own coming into wisdom. And so, in March 1993, nine of us met on the Eastern Shore of Maryland for the weekend, and we've been croning together ever since.

In addition to them, there are three other very special Crones in my life to whom this book is dedicated. They are women whose lives are so extraordinary in the example they set, and so rich with the possibilities of female energy, intellect, and spirit, that I consider it one of the greatest gifts of my life that each, in her eighties, became my friend.

It seemed only natural, then, that when I thought about a title for my book of stories about women coming into their own wisdom, it should honor the Crones I know and love as well as all those I don't. So for all the Albertas, Elizabeths, and Esthers, and for my special group, this one is for you. Long may we crone!

✦ ✧ ✦

Croning Tales

DEBRA
✦ ◇ ✦
Mothers

Of all the features of the pleasant little room in which Debra is lying, the wall clock is most prominent to her. Its round face beams the reassuring passage of time straight at her whenever she opens her eyes, assuring her that something is happening. Simultaneously, it irritates her that only five or ten minutes have elapsed from one time check to another. As though the clock were the face of an annoying acquaintance, Debra forces herself to look away, first at the Picasso mother and child print to her left, then at the pastel flowered curtains next to it, and then to the fetal monitor in the corner of the room. Her eyes wander to the doorway as if at any moment Michael will come bounding in, even though she knows he couldn't possibly make it from the West Coast for another three hours. But always her eyes come to rest on the clock, which is for her a metaphor for the whole of the birthing room.

She has been there for two hours now, but still her labor is not very difficult. It is being two weeks early that has prompted Polly, her nurse-midwife, to admit her at this stage. Damned irritating, she thinks. Just what she imagined would happen when she and Michael had argued about his leaving on business this close to her due date. "I'll be back in time, no sweat," he had said cavalierly. "This is too damned important a meeting for me to miss." Then, "Deb, be reasonable. It's two whole weeks before you're due. I need to go to this meeting." She had agreed reluctantly, not acknowledging even to herself how angry she felt.

The whole of her pregnancy had angered her in one way or another. It had come at the wrong time, for a start. "I wanted to finish my thesis first!" she had wailed to Michael when Polly confirmed her suspicions. "Besides, we aren't ready financially."

Sometimes she didn't know why she felt so enraged and unsettled. "Hormones," Polly said, but they both knew there was more to it than that, deep down, where she couldn't touch it.

Now, between contractions, Debra closes her eyes, fading into that half-state of being that allows the mind to wander into bizarre and remote territory. For what seems like hours, she floats between the present and events in her past, brought out of her reverie only by a contraction or the compulsion to look again at the clock as though its lethargic movement is the only reassurance that Michael will come, her labor will end, and her child will be born.

Funny about time, she muses to herself. How it can absolutely creep on some occasions, and yet fly by other of life's larger events. Here she is, twenty-eight and giving birth to her first child, while the events of her life, save one, seem to have passed so quickly that she has not paused to appreciate them, or to contemplate their meaning.

She thinks most about her mother's life, not her own. There will be time to understand the forces shaping her, but it is urgent to understand her mother, not that she ever will altogether. Perhaps one needs absolute objectivity for that, she thinks. But how can one remain objective about one's own mother, she wonders drowsily, especially in view of what happened?

The contraction that rouses her suddenly grips her abdomen with new force. She is glad to see Polly re-enter the room. After a quick check, Polly says cheerfully, "Well, things are progressing!"

"God, I hope Michael gets here soon! He's never here when I need him!"

"Debra, be fair," Polly says firmly. "Don't keep taking it out on Michael."

"You're right! You're right. I've got to stop doing that. How far am I?"

"Eight centimeters. Coming into transition. That's why you're getting edgy."

"Yeah? Well here's another one!" Debra groans, grasping Polly's hand.

"Okay, let's breathe. Look at me! Relax, and breathe!" When the contraction has subsided, Debra looks gratefully at her friend, releasing her grip on Polly's hand.

"God, I'm glad you're here, Pol. This is getting rough."

"You're doing fine."

"I wonder what kind of labor my mother had with me. We never talked about it. I always imagine it must have been pretty gruesome, or she would have had more kids. There were so many things she never told me . . ."

"Debra, don't."

"I want my mother, Polly. I want my mother to be here with me! I want her to be my baby's grandmother. I want to tell her that I loved her. I want to know why she did it."

Another contraction interrupts.

"Your job right now is to have this baby," Polly says.

When Michael arrives, Debra is in the final stages of labor.

"There's nothing to worry about," Polly reassures him. She puts her hand on his arm. "Michael, she's on edge. Don't be surprised if she's hard on you. She's thinking a lot about her mom."

"Thanks," Michael says, patting Polly's hand. Then he enters the birthing room.

"Hi, Sweetheart." He smiles, bending down to kiss her lips. "I'm here now. How are you holding up?"

"God, Michael! I just want it to be over. When will it be over?" she pants, squeezing his hand.

"Soon, Sweetie. Soon. All in good time."

"God! You sound just like my mother. That's what she always said. It was always 'All in good time' when I was a kid!"

"Maybe she was right," Michael says firmly.

"Yeah. She was always right. Except for the one big time when she was wrong."

"Debra, when are you going to forgive your mother? It's been seven years."

"I know. I'm sorry! God, I'm glad you're here, Michael. I do love you."

"I love you too, Debra."

"Here comes another one!"

Debra's contractions intensify, but still she closes her eyes during the brief respite between pains, releasing them reluctantly from the clock, which becomes more personified each time she lets go of its face. Fading into semi-sleep for the minute or two of relief as Michael rubs the small of her back or strokes her cheek, she begins to forget where she is until the jolt of a new pain shocks her into wakefulness like an electric prod. The sensation is not unlike what she experiences whenever she remembers her mother's death, and it brings with it nausea and a revulsion that makes her want to flee.

But she cannot escape. Not her labor, nor her memory, nor her guilt.

Everyone said at the time, of course, that she should bear no guilt. She was a good daughter, had done everything a good girl should do. Still, there were moments she remembers, so exaggerated and wretched in her mind's eye that she can barely look back on them even now.

"You're going to push me too far one of these days!" her mother had cried when she was being a difficult child.

"Don't push!" Polly's voice comes through the fog of pain.

"I didn't push her! I didn't push her!"

* * * * *

The ticking of the clock is so pronounced suddenly that it seems to chant, "Don't go. Don't go. Oh, no! Oh, no!"

"Oh, no! Oh, my God, no!" Debra, eyes squeezed shut, sees her mother again on the window ledge, one leg in and the other out. It had happened as soon as she opened the door to her mother's apartment. The airiness of the living room, despite its small size, had seemed a welcome greeting at first. But then, like a Plexiglas wall, the fresh air blowing the sheers gaily toward her seemed a grotesque barrier keeping her from passing the infinite distance of a few yards separating her from her mother. "Oh my God! Mom! Don't move! Please don't! We'll talk. Please don't move!" Inching all the while toward the abyss.

"It's too late for talk, Debra."

"Look, I know you've been down. God knows I haven't done all I could have. But we can work things out. We can work things out, Ma, I promise you."

"No! I've made up my mind!"

"Look, I know Daddy hasn't exactly been . . . well, good to you, and . . . "

"And now you're gone, out on your own. What've I got left? Debra, I'm so miserable."

And then, suddenly, with a force unknown to her ever before, Debra feels the power of a river bursting forth from her groins, drenching her in warm, wet, oddly comforting streams which escape from their source in gushes of liberation. Now she opens her eyes to the faceless clock, and the sound of Polly and Michael in unison.

"Okay! Now you can push!"

She has heard such animal sounds only once before, and realized then too that they came from within herself. Now, again, deep, cavernous wails escape the depth of her being, and as her own child forces its way into life, Debra's guttural sounds echo those she had made as her mother's hand slipped from hers. Then, the horror of what was happening washed over her like a tidal wave of such enormous proportions that her entire being was sucked into it and only by the most exquisite exercise of will could she keep from tumbling after. But now, once more called upon for an act of willful exertion, she lets go, yielding this time to the flow of life and her long urgency for release, for the giving up of pain and guilt and rage. And welcoming rebirth, she brings forth, in a wet warm river, her daughter, whose newborn wail, infinitely smaller and sweeter than her own, fills the room.

When she opens her eyes, she sees that Michael is crying, and that their infant daughter has been placed across her abdomen. But only after the baby is in Debra's arms, and Michael has gone home to rest, does she think to look at the clock on the wall, whose midnight hands seem poised in prayer. Then she hears its gentle ticking once again, sure and steady, like the encouragement of a good friend. Only then does she give way to sleep in deep and peaceful repose, free at last of half-dreams and gnawing memory. And only then does she dream her mother, smiling silently over Debra and her new daughter.

JULIE
✦ ✧ ✦
When Witches Laugh

What exactly does it sound like when someone has a nervous breakdown?" Julie sits beside her father in the black Buick, her feet extending over the seat just far enough so that the ruffles on her socks touch its edge. She stares at her Mary Jane patent leather shoes, then fingers the bow of her left one.

"Sit back," her father says.

"But what does it sound like?" This time she looks at him.

"It doesn't sound like anything," he says, glancing into the rearview mirror. It's not like a machine, or something."

"Why do they call it a breakdown then? What happens?"

"It's . . . it's sort of like getting worn out, and being so tired you just have to lay down . . . I guess."

He puts his hand on the knot of his necktie, and looks again into the rearview mirror, even though no one travels the rural road on a Sunday, unless they are going to Alcona to visit someone.

"Your mother's had a lot on her mind lately. She's just tired. She'll be all right."

"So then why couldn't she just stay home and rest?"

"It's hard to explain, Julie. When you're a little older, you'll understand." He pauses. "But your mom needs to see you."

Julie looks out the window. For a long time they ride in silence, except for her father's sighs, and the sound of the wind in the naked maple trees, like a whisk broom on leather.

The hospital sits back from the main road. From the long, narrow access road it looks like a castle, or a palace, its turreted corners spewing naked ivy vines across the brick walls. Directly in front, a garden, which spells "Alcona State Hospital" in summer, lies fallow now. In front of the garden, a small lake shelters the remnants of water lilies, limp and frail, like the remains of a shipwreck.

Julie watches her father as he searches for a parking place. He licks his bottom lip, draws in a long breath, and sighs enormously. She imitates his motions, pressing her tongue against her lip until it is moist. Then she inhales, letting the air go noisily. He looks at her and smiles. When they are out of the car he says, "Julie, this might not be easy. But just remember, no matter what, Mom loves you."

She looks at him quizzically, her eyes moving up his slender figure until they rest on his face. Then she puts her hand into his. It is warm and clammy, and when he smiles again, she sees that he has beads of sweat on his upper lip, even though it is cold outside. She shivers and moves closer into him.

In the entrance hall, a slightly antiseptic smell suggests a hospital, while large plants and overstuffed chairs make the cavernous space seem more like a deserted hotel lobby. Around a coffee urn a calligraphied note hangs limp. "Help Yourself," it says, but there are no more cups. A receptionist is seated behind a glass window. She slides the window open, her mouth curving into a red crescent smile, as if her face has been carefully hand painted onto porcelain. Her eyes look glassily at Julie. "May I help you?" she asks.

"It's all right," Julie's father says. "I know the way."

"If there's anything . . . "

"We're fine. Thank you."

They enter the elevator. Julie still clutches her father's hand as she looks down at her patent leather shoes. Then, head tilted back, she follows the floors as they light up above the elevator door. Two-three-four-five-six-seven. At seven they get out.

Another receptionist with wire frame glasses perched on her nose says, "East or West?"

"West."

The receptionist rises, reaches for a ring of keys at her waist, and, peering through her round glasses to find the right one, opens the metal doors to their left. Julie looks at her father, but he only clears his throat.

"Why . . . "

"Sssssh . . . "

The first thing they both see is a woman inching her way along the wall. Back pressed flat, palms of her hands feeling the grainy paint before she will slide further, she moves first one foot, then the other. Her eyes dart left, then right, and her unwashed white hair, matted with oil, falls across her face like a dirty lace curtain. Then another woman appears.

"What the hell do you want?" she sneers at Julie.

A nurse appears from somewhere. "Now, Mrs. Pickett, why don't we just come down to the activities room, hmm?" she coddles, putting a starched white-coated arm around the woman. Her rubber-soled shoes make a rhythmic squeaking sound as they move away.

"Fuck you, bitch."

Julie's father puts his arm around her shoulder. Another nurse looks at him, then at Julie. Julie sees the same look in her eyes as in the downstairs receptionist's. She licks her bottom lip as she did in the car, this time moving her tongue faster.

"Where's Mom?" she whispers.

Her mother's room is the last one on the endless corridor. Its white walls are interrupted only by a framed print of Monet's *Water Lilies*, their blue-greens forming a blur against the starkly vacant canvas of the room. The windows are large, with chicken wire over them. The bed is firmly made. Her mother sits in a solitary chair by the window. When they enter, she turns slowly toward them, but says nothing.

Julie, still clutching her father's hand, looks up at her mother. "Hi," she whispers.

"Sarah!" her father says. "Here's a surprise for you."

"Oh." Sarah's eyes are blank. "Hello."

"How are you? You're looking well! Julie's come to see you."

"Yes."

"She has lots to tell you. Don't you, Julie? Tell Mom about your birthday party."

"I'm having a sleepover."

"Is it your birthday already?"

"Yeah. Don't you remember?" Julie stares at her mother's eyes, which are watching her hands trace the stitched edge of a handkerchief. When her mother doesn't answer, she goes on.

"There are six kids, but Theresa can't come. Dad said we could get a pizza, and Aunt Helen is going to make a cake." She pauses, wraps her right Mary Jane behind her left ankle until it locks tight against the front of her left leg. "Do you think you might be home by next Saturday?"

"Mom's going to have a nice long, quiet rest, so that when she comes home again, she'll be her old self," her father says, putting his hand on Julie's shoulder.

Then he turns to his wife. "How are you, Sarah?"

"I don't like the treatments."

"I know. But the doctors say . . . "

"You said I wouldn't have to have them." Her lips are rigid, and she fumbles with the handkerchief in her lap. "We agreed."

"Yes. But Dr. Joseph said . . . We want you well again. Don't we, Julie?" He looks at the floor. "You'll be feeling fine in no time and then this will all be behind us."

Julie's mother looks out the window. "We agreed." She puts the handkerchief to her mouth. "It looks cold outside. It's getting dark. You should go home now."

"We can stay a little longer."

"No. Take Julie home. She probably has homework to do."

"But it's winter break."

"Oh, is it?" her mother asks vaguely. "I lose all track of time here."

"We'll come back soon."

Julie's father bends to kiss his wife. She raises her cheek to him. Then Julie moves closer to her. When her mother does not open her arms, Julie touches her mother's hair. "I love you, Mom," she says.

Julie and her father walk down the long hallway in silence, their heads bent as if in prayer. At the metal doors, several women in cotton flowered gunnysack dresses and paper slippers shuffle to touch the door as they say goodbye to their visitors. Suddenly, one of them screeches, "It's all your fault! You put me in here! Damn you to hell!" A nurse restrains her. The receptionist, waiting with her keys for the last visitors to exit, smiles weakly.

"How could she forget it was my birthday? My tenth birthday?" The car is cold and Julie shivers. Her father is silent. "Dad?"

Silence.

"I know what it sounds like now."

"What, Julie?"

"The sound of someone having a nervous breakdown." She faces her father. "It sounds like when witches laugh. And the worst part is, nobody can make them stop, no fairy godmother, not even God."

Tears peak in her eyes and slip over onto her cheeks, but she presses her tongue onto her bottom lip to stop them. "And the really worst part about it is, I think once you hear it, it never, ever goes away."

Her father turns the key, presses the gas pedal to the floor until the black Buick spits out angry fumes, and backs out of the parking space onto the macadam, grown icy with the approaching darkness.

HELGA
✦ ✧ ✦
Helga's Day

"Mornin' to you, Mrs. Cameron!" says Wickham, the milkman, peering through the open kitchen window. "How many pints today?"

"The usual, Mr. Wickham. Not too many guests this morning," says Helga, as she cracks another egg into the bowl, pausing to push a strand of blonde hair out of her eyes with the back of her hand.

"Good day to you now," says Wickham.

"Yes," says Helga, neither looking up nor smiling. "And to you, Mr. Wickham."

She counts the yokes. Ten. That should be enough for the four scrambled. She takes the hand beater from the peg on the wall and begins to beat the eggs. "Whiry, whiry, weary, weary," the beater chants. She pours the egg batter into the hot skillet and stirs with the spatula. With her other hand, Helga pops the toast down and gives the three fried eggs a shake so they won't stick to the frying pan. When the scrambled eggs are ready, she takes seven plates from the warmer and arranges bacon, eggs, toast, and tomato slices. Picking up two at a time with the corners of a tea towel, she glances at her reflection in the window and enters the dining room, surveying the guests.

The three students from Glasgow, drab and quiet, don't interest her. It's the American family that attracts her attention, especially the woman, who speaks softly to her children about the things they will see today. Helga thought once that she might be like her, with manicured nails and crisp clothes, on holiday with her family. It seems now a silly thing to have imagined.

"Here we are then!" she announces cheerily, making two quick return trips to the kitchen for the remaining eggs. "Now, more tea? Coffee? Can I get you anything else?"

"No, I think we're fine!" vote the occupants of the two tables, looking up from their maps and guidebooks.

"Lovely countryside!" says the American man.

"Yes," says Helga wistfully, "I'm glad you like it. I'm sorry about the rain. That's the trouble with the Lake District. All this rain . . . "

"Well, never mind. That's what makes it so lovely!"

"Yes, I suppose. It certainly doesn't seem to stop people coming to these parts. Of course, they can leave after a few days, can't they?"

"Mummy!"

"Oh, excuse me. I'll just go and see to the children."

Helga grasps the bannister and pulls herself upstairs. "Yes, Bridget, I'm just coming. Martin, can you help with Brian? They're going to be late for school."

"Yes, Luv. Just 'avin' a bit o' trouble getting up this morning. Must be the rain. I'm all stiff-like today."

"All right, then. I'll do it. Can you check up on the guests, then? See they've paid up and everything."

By the time she has brushed Bridget's hair, tied Brian's shoes, put them in their rain macks, made sure they have their lunches, and sent them up the street, Martin is engaged in conversation with the American family. Helga sits on the bottom stair, wipes her hands on her soiled apron, and rests her head against the bannister to listen.

"I been to America," Martin is saying. "Got me one o' them Greyhound bus tickets. I'll never forget. Went to the station in New York and said I was goin' to Florida. On that bus three days, I was!" chuckles Martin. "I thought it'd be about three hours!"

"You like to travel then, do you?" asks the American man, polite, interested.

"Me? Oh, yeah. Would a' kept doin' it, too, but then I met Helga. She's Danish, you know. Met her in Denmark when I was in the Merchant Marine. We got married, had the kids, and that was that."

Helga comes into the dining room, smoothing her apron, and Martin retreats to the kitchen. She busies herself clearing the dishes, smiling with her mouth but not her eyes. The American woman looks deeply at Helga's face, with its big blue emotionless eyes and pink face, early-lined. "It must be hard work running a bed and breakfast. You must be 'on' all the time."

"Yes, 'tis. But it's not all that bad, really. We do alright. Better than Liverpool. We tried Liverpool for a year and a half. When that didn't work out, I thought, why not try doing a B&B? At least that way, I'd meet a lot of interesting people. All the coming and going, well, it almost gives you the feeling you've been somewhere yourself. We've done okay, really. Maybe one of these days, we'll even get a bit of holiday ourselves. A couple of days in London. That's what I'd like."

The American woman understands, and wishes she could get up and help the weary Helga with the washing up. Helga knows she understands, and hurries to the kitchen before revealing any more. In the kitchen, a fleeting faintness makes her grab the edge of the sink. She fills the basin with hot water and tells Martin to go out and be sure the vacancy sign is up. As she begins to wash dishes, hot tears fight their way to the back of her eyes like a dormant volcano with new lava to spill. She sees herself, poor and pretty, a young girl on a small farm in Denmark, and remembers Martin in dress uniform, dashing and virile before the accident at the Liverpool docks rendered him snarled and shrunken. Poor Martin, she thinks. It isn't his fault. A dreamer dragged down. Maybe life would have been different, if only he hadn't been injured, if the children hadn't come so soon, if . . . Mustn't think about it. Wouldn't have been any better back home. At least Martin had offered her hope in a new country. Who was to know? He did his best, poor fellow, and they were making a decent go of it with the B&B. Perhaps one day they would make enough to hire some help. Martin pops his head in. "The Americans are leavin', Luv. Should I collect?"

"It's alright. I'll see to it. You go and have a rest. Later on, you can help me do the beds."

Helga makes change for the Americans. "I hope you have a lovely holiday."

"You take care," says the woman, like a worried mother. "Try to get those few days in London."

When they have gone, Helga strips all the beds, and remakes them without disturbing Martin, who dozes in his TV chair. She cleans each of the bathrooms and makes a laundry parcel ready for pickup. Afterwards, she eats a piece of stale bread with some cheese and drinks cold tea from her morning's cup before setting off to the village with her wicker basket and change purse. Up the High Street she nips into the general store, quickly loading her basket with eggs, bacon, juice, tomatoes, and bread for tomorrow's breakfast. There's still enough in the larder for their supper tonight, so when the shopkeeper says "That be all today?" she nods, smiles tentatively.

She arrives home in time to make three bookings for the night before setting out tea for Martin and the children, who will be home from school any minute. "I'll just have a quick bath," she tells Martin, savoring the fifteen minutes to herself.

She emerges from the bathroom just as Bridget and Brian burst through the door. "Hello, my darlings. Come and tell me all about your day. Did you have a nice day?" Over tea, Martin and Helga listen to schoolyard gossip, smiling once to each other. Then, as the children draw stick figures at the kitchen table and Martin checks the paper for "help wanted," Helga brings out last night's leftovers to reheat for dinner. She bathes the children while Martin sets the kitchen table.

Later, after supper, she reads a story before tucking the youngsters in. Martin watches television, dozing. "Go to bed," she tells him softly. "I'll just set up the dining room before the guests arrive."

The first lot arrive at ten. The others soon follow. Tonight they are a French couple, maybe on honeymoon, an elderly German and his wife, and an English family of three. Helga shows them each to their rooms, working out in her head if she's got enough bacon and eggs and how much they will make tonight. She offers tea, but they all decline. "Well, I'll say goodnight then," she says, withdrawing from the second floor.

She checks the children, who sleep like angels in a museum painting. Then she locks the front door and puts out all but the nightlight. In their room, Martin snores softly from the double bed. Helga undresses, slips on her flannel nightdress and slides silently under the covers. She arches her back until the ache at the base of her spine begins to recede. She would have liked to sit quietly by herself for a few minutes, sipping warm milk and reading. But five-thirty will come early in the morning. God, I hope it's a nice day, she thinks, rolling over and pulling the covers around her ear. Maybe then it won't be so hard to get up.

Martin snorts, and it begins to rain. The drops on the windowpane drip down like elongated tears distorted by shadows cast from the street lamp. Helga closes her eyes, wonders where the American woman is tonight, and waits for sleep to come.

SONDRA
◆ ◇ ◆
Standing Up to Eugene

I know 'zactly when it was I decided to do it. Didn't know how, or when — jus' knew I would do it. It was when he told me to shut up.

"Shut up!" he said. "You jus' bein' stupid." Right there in front of my children, and my brother James, who jus' stood there, saying nothin'. Later on, he tried tellin' me that Eugene was jus' feelin' upset, bein' 'round death like that and all, but I didn't wanna hear it. Not after I'd been tryin' to sound some encouragement. And besides, he ain't just a pussycat having a temper tantrum now and again. He talks like that to me, and the kids, all the time. I was gettin' downright tired of it.

Not that I haven't wanted to put a stop to it before now. Lotsa times I wanted to tell that man where to get off, but I couldn't seem to do it. I'd always get a feelin' in my stomach like as if I was 'bout to fall off a cliff, or get hurt in some kinda big way. Not that Eugene ever laid a hand on me. He wouldn't do that. Didn't have to. His words hurt me jus' as bad.

Sometimes me and my friends would sit around talking about men, the way they act, and treat their women, and it seemed like all of us had the same to contend with one way and another. But then a few of them would say to me, "Sondra, why you lettin' that man treat you that way? He got no call to be talkin' to you like that." Well, easy for them to say. They only came 'round when he wasn't there.

I guess it was pretty much the same for all of us. Married young, a house full of kids before you know where you're at, and there you are. A woman gotta have time and money and an empty laundry basket before she can be free.

Still, it started wearin' on me a long time ago, the way Eugene acts. Always poutin' and snappin' 'bout somethin' or other. Never seein' a good thing in anybody, least of all my friends and relations.

That's why I knew there'd be trouble the minute I said I was takin' Ida Mae in after she got outta the hospital.

"What you mean, girl?" Eugene said, his eyes gettin' big and black as two pieces of coal. "We got 'nough mouths to feed here!"

"I know. But we'll find a way. I won't let her go into no home or nothin', after all she's done for me."

"Look, I know she helped raise you and all that, but I don't want to hear no more 'bout it, you hear?"

I looked him in the eye like I don't do very often and I said, "Ida Mae is dyin' and she ain't gonna die nowhere else but here." Then I walked to the bathroom and got diarrhea 'cause my stomach gets upset whenever I be scared.

I still didn't know yet that I was gonna do it, but I figured havin' Ida Mae 'round would make some kinda difference in my life, just like it did when I was a kid. It was just a feelin', but I was right 'bout that. Once I got her home from the hospital, there was only two ways to describe Eugene: mean and extra mean. At least I knew what to expect every time he walked in the door. I just knew that everythin' out of his mouth was goin' to be some kinda insult or demand. "What the hell's this?" he'd say, pickin' up the light bill. "Can't you keep those damn kids quiet?" "Christ, this place is in a mess!"

Well, what'd he expect with everythin' I was trying to keep up with, and no help from him. No help at all. Just his hot, sweaty body pushing at me at night like some kinda goddamn machine that couldn't figure out the other half of it was broken down long time ago.

If it was just me, who knows what woulda happened. Maybe I'd have done it sooner, or maybe not at all. But it was watchin' how he talked to the kids, and how he wouldn't say a word to poor Ida Mae, that made me know I was gettin' close to the edge. "Can't you be civil?" I said to him one day, that feelin' creepin' up into my stomach. "Maybe it would help Ida Mae to get better." And that was when he said it to me, right in front of James and the kids.

"Shut up! You jus' bein' stupid."

And that was 'zactly when I knew I was gonna do it.

Course, I still didn't know when, or how it would come 'bout. But I knew that when I found my chance, I'd take it. "One man's extremity is another woman's opportunity," Ida Mae used to say to me. She was always sayin' things like that. "Walk tall, and be proud you a woman," she'd tell me when I was a slumpin' 'round teenager. "What goes 'round comes 'round." I never could figure that one out. But she had an expression for everythin', and somehow, just bein' in a room with her made me feel like even my life was worth somethin'.

That was how it was even with her so frail and dyin' now. She would half sit up in the bed after I got done bathin' her and combin' her thin wisps of gray hair, and crossin' her bony hands in front of her, she'd look straight at me with those eyes, grayed over with cataracts, and see through everythin' still.

"You grew to be a good woman," she said to me one day.

"Maybe I'm good, but I don't guess you think I'm so smart."

"Why you say that, child?"

"Ida Mae, you no fool. You can see what goes on 'round here. If I'da been smart, I wouldn'ta been stuck in my . . . situation."

"Honey, there's lotsa women stuck in that same situation. Maybe things are changin' now, what with all them movements for this and that, girls nowadays gettin' smarter. But in my day, and yours, we did what we thought we had to do. Marryin' a big, handsome man like Eugene seemed like the right thing. Bein' a missus with some kids is what made us feel important, respectable. By the time we got it figured out that the only respect we had was the respect we came with, we all felt trapped, and crazy-like. What you gotta do is hang on to that respect you was born with. Ain't nobody can take that away from you, less you willin' to give it up."

"Ida Mae, you always did make me feel like a real person. No wonder my momma loved you like a real sister. I don't know what I would've done without you after she passed. And all you gave up for us, too."

"You mean not gettin' married to a Eugene? Girl, what you think I am, crazy!"

And then sick as she was, we laughed and laughed till the tears came down our cheeks like rain after a dry spell.

I could see that Ida Mae was fadin' fast, and she knew it too. But there was some kinda joy in havin' her there, and bein' together. A sort of peacefulness laid over the house, long as Eugene wasn't there. Even the kids noticed it. "Momma," they'd say when they'd come home from school and gone up to her room for a visit, "Ida Mae isn't gonna die real soon, is she?"

"Only when her time come," I'd say, givin' them a hug.

Eugene could see that her time was comin' too, only he was glad of it. He wanted her outta the house, mostly 'cause he knew that havin' her there was makin' some kinda magic between us. He was just as jealous as if I was carryin' on with another man, but what's more, he was downright scared, 'cause he just couldn't figure out how two women, one of them nearly dead, could have so much pass between 'em. After a while, it got to be a joke.

"That Eugene, he thinks you're a witch," I'd tell Ida Mae while I rubbed her back to ease the pain.

"Well, honey, he don't know the half of it!"

Maybe Eugene was right, 'cause sure as I breathe, somethin' mighty powerful was creepin' up inside of me, and one way or 'nother, I knew it was comin' from Ida Mae.

I kept havin' that feelin' even after she slipped into a coma and the doctor said it wouldn't be more than a few more days. Even when it was only me talkin', I felt her strength somehow comin' up around me. And even though the doctor said she couldn't hear me, I know she could, and I do believe her hand kept squeezin' mine right up to the end.

I believe it was the squeeze of her hand that finally made me do it.

I'd been sittin' by the bed for hours that night, knowin' it was nearly over, when Eugene came in, lookin' clenched and angry.

"Girl, you been in this room day and night. It's enough. I want her outta here — Now! She ain't gonna know no difference whether she's here or in a hospital. Your duty is to the livin', not this old lady. I'm callin' for the ambulance to get her."

"No!"

"What you say?"

"I said no."

"Well, it ain't for you to decide."

"Eugene, I said NO! You hear me? Ida Mae is my family and she is not leavin' here while she is drawin' breath. You got that?"

"You bitch! Just who the hell you think you're talkin' to?"

"I thought I was talkin' to my husband. Someone who's supposed to care for me and mine. Although God only knows why I should still think like that after all these years. You been comin' between me and everyone I care about long as I can remember. You jus' can't stand it, can you, Eugene, when I'm feelin' strong and good 'bout something? Always got to be punishin' me, don't you?"

Eugene looked at me then like I'd gone completely crazy. But it was his face that looked like someone who'd gone to the other side. Then I saw him make a fist, and grit his teeth so hard his jawbone stuck out on each side.

"Go 'head. Why don't you hit me, Eugene? That's what you wanna do, isn't it? Been beatin' up on me with your words and your attitude all these years, might as well jus' go 'head and hit me. Wouldn't surprise nobody, 'cause you're just a two-bit bully, and everybody knows it."

Then his jaw fell open and his eyes kinda rolled up in his head, and he turned and walked out of the room. And then I realized that I was still squeezin' Ida Mae's hand, and that she had an expression on her face that surely did resemble a smile. But that wasn't what surprised me most. What really shocked me was that my stomach felt just fine.

Ida Mae died the next day. Early, early in the morning she just slipped peacefully into the next world while I was holdin' her hand. I sent the children next door while I made the arrangements and washed and dressed her little body. When the time came for them to take her from the house, I had me a good cry. Then I got myself freshened up and went for the children so as they could have a proper goodbye with her too.

The house is terrible lonely without her now. But me and the kids feel her spirit with us, and we talk about her a lot, laughin' at all the funny things she used to say. That feels good 'cause, like Ida Mae always said, so long as you talk about the dead, they aren't really gone from you.

Things are a whole lot better without Eugene 'round, that's for sure. He left the night before Ida Mae died, just after I told him where to get off, and he never did come back. I hear from James he's livin' with a friend from work. I don't know what he plans to do, but he knows, and I know, that whether or not he comes back, things 'round here gonna be mighty different from now on.

I started sellin' some of my handiwork to make ends meet, and just the other day, some lady from a department store downtown called to ask if I could start makin' a lot more for her, so I guess I'll be alright, one way and another.

One thing I do know for sure, though. Life seems a whole lot more full of possibility ever since I stood up to Eugene. And that's jus' one more thing I got to be grateful to Ida Mae for, even though if she were here, she wouldn't take an ounce of credit for it. But that don't matter. Only thing that matters is that she'd be proud of me, and that I'm proud of myself.

And that's a whole lot more than Eugene can say.

JILL
✦ ✧ ✦
Seaplane

On her third day of self-imposed retreat, Jill's solitude is broken again by the little pink airplane that soars above the tree line each day, its noisy motor assaulting her thoughts. The plane mesmerizes her with its twists and turns. A fatalistic streak in her feels sure it will fail and, overcome by a subtle, almost perverse sensation, she wants to be there when it happens. Something in that event seems inevitable.

Each morning, after walking from her room in the annex to the original portion of the old hotel, Jill eats breakfast before hiking to the far side of the lake, where sooner or later the pink plane ascends. First she likes to pause on the long expanse of porch which wraps around the whitewashed and turreted old chateau, taking in the scene before her. Just below, a terraced veranda lined with wicker rocking chairs looks out over the lake, large and deep blue like an enormous sapphire spawning tiny diamond baguettes. In the middle of the lake, a small tree-covered island rises up like a policeman, guiding boat and seaplane traffic in orderly one-way patterns. Rowboats and canoes glide silently by, disappearing behind the island. Bright yellow paddleboats and multi-colored sailfish dot the lake's edges. The occasional roar of a seaplane engine interrupts the tranquility with its impending liftoff, but otherwise, it is serene.

On the terrace, senior citizens in colorful cardigans and sunhats watch as their grandchildren gather at the foot of the lake each morning for day camp, shouting and jumping up and down in their gaily colored swimsuits to demand the attention of counselors, or their parents who have staked out chaise lounges further along the lake by tossing bright beach towels on them. The view is the perfect backdrop for a film of *The White Hotel*, a novel in which an odd assortment of people vacation in a hotel overlooking a lake while a set of bizarre events takes over their lives.

But for its beauty, the lakeside hotel, stately and old-world elegant, is an unlikely place for someone like Jill to vacation alone. But she has felt a deep need to be on her own, to "sort it out," as her best friend, Chloe, put it, "before it becomes a mental health issue." Jill recognizes the growing brittleness in herself, the lowered energy, a sense of aimlessness in the year since Andrew has gone. It frightens her. She feels confused and weary.

Making her way around the lake to the small deserted beach where she waits for the seaplane, Jill reflects on her state of mind. She misses Andrew deeply, recalls their good moments and relinquishes the conflicts that drove them apart in the end. But it isn't just losing Andrew. It is also boredom, malaise. True, she has moved up the ladder as senior editor in one of New York's major publishing houses, gone there because academia was driving her mad. It doesn't help, of course, that forty looms on the horizon, that magic number that makes her snap at an editor, "If I get one more proposal for the ultimate work on baby boomers and their biological clocks, I'm going to scream!"

But that's not it, she thinks now, settling onto a canvas chaise to await the pink plane's punctuation of her thoughts. At least not all of it. There's something else going on. I've been bored with work before, lost lovers, faced change. When I wanted something, I made it happen. Change! Lights! Camera! Action! A career a year if that's what it took to keep me stimulated. "Can't play the game the way other people do, Chloe. I'm the creative type, you know." Well, Christ! Let's face it, she admonishes herself. No one can keep up like that. Where does the energy come from? How much risk-taking can one person survive?

Jill gets up and paces the deserted beach. She feels agitated, like a teenager stood up at the movie theater because the seaplane hasn't appeared yet. She decides to canoe into the lake. The paddling helps work off her irritation. Donning a life jacket, she slides the green vessel silently into the water, and climbs in. Canoeing soothes her. She loves sliding across the water, in quiet, calm movement, confident and directed. The rhythmic motion of paddling helps to pace her thinking.

She lets her thoughts flow freely, letting go of tension and angst. Then, she allows the canoe to drift toward the center of the lake. The sun plays on the rippling water. A slight breeze stirs the birch trees lining the lake, and a family of ducks paddles purposefully at the water's edge. Pulling the paddles in, she settles into the curve of the boat's floor, resting her head against the seat to wait for the seaplane. Again, her thoughts turn inward, inspired by the motion of the canoe on the water as though a great Indian matriarch is lulling her toward self-discovery. She thinks of the therapy sessions with Peter just after Andrew had gone. Wise, gentle Peter. How loved he made her feel as they worked together toward centeredness, balance, what he liked to call "letting go." And how difficult it was for her, product of insecure immigrant parents, East Coast overachievement, self-compulsion, this letting go business! But for the moment, she manages to achieve some semblance of it, and a smile crosses her face, softening her dark features so that in the mirror of her mind, she sees herself once again as vibrant and beautiful. What a classic Pisces, she thinks with a return of her native humor — here I am, adrift in a rudderless ship.

And then she hears its din. Shading her eyes with her hand, she lifts herself up to scout the sky for the pink craft, realizing suddenly that a surge of excitement has made her breathing rapid and uneven.

It comes toward her from the other side of the tiny island in the middle of the lake. Its little engine snorts and groans, and in the glare of the sun, the craft looks like a beleaguered butterfly, coughing and sputtering. Jill marvels at its fragility. It looks to be no more than a paper airplane that children make, only with a real engine. But its shrill color and its arrogant maneuvering belie its tenuousness, and it is this that endears it to her. Its daring is enviable.

She has begun to believe, to hope perhaps, that as she finds the craft magnetic, it too seeks her. Now as it comes toward her, direct and determined, her fantasy is reinforced. And in this odd sense of communing, she feels somehow empowered, freed from a weightiness, as if the levity of the plane is bestowed on her own being. Now, as it draws closer, she begins to feel that whoever is piloting has indeed noticed her. The plane's action seems thoroughly and forcefully guided toward her. She waits. In a minute it will pass over her, if it doesn't veer off in another direction. But steady it comes, and passing directly over her, it tips its wing in a gesture unmistakable in its definiteness before disappearing over the mountain behind her. A smile crosses her lips. She has the odd sensation of feeling both titillated and silly at once. The tipped wing, like a wink, a flirtation, makes her feel girlish. But more than that, an unaccountable sense of freedom envelops her. She cannot explain it. Nor does she wish to examine it. She chooses, rather, to enjoy it, as it wraps around her like a cloak of daisies on a spring morning.

She maintains this ebullience through the day. But later, Jill dreams a recurring dream. She sees herself standing at the chain-link fence of an airport. Anticipation is high around her. She remains calm and quiet, even knowing what is about to occur. She tells no one in the dream. In her variations on this dream, Jill never boards the fatal plane herself, nor does she ever allow anyone she loves to do so. But when the accident happens, she — and only she — is composed, calm, able to cope in the midst of the chaos and grief around her, because she has known it would happen. On this night, the plane she watches engulfed in flames is the pink seaplane. And the only one aboard is the daring, faceless pilot.

The next morning, Jill lingers long on the terrace after breakfast, brooding over her dream. That this version centered on the pink seaplane does not seem surprising, and it is not that fact upon which she dwells. Rather, she thinks about the dream itself, which she has not experienced in a long time. Finding herself unable to explore it insightfully, she decides to call Chloe.

"What do you make of it?" she asks.

"Well, I don't know. I expect Freud would have a heyday. Control, you know, and all that Psych 101 crap."

"Exactly. I mean, I'm not sure I care what it all means. But why am I so fixated on that silly plane? It's ridiculous, really."

"Not if it's working for you. Getting you where you need to be somehow."

"Christ, Chloe, how can I get where I need to be, as you put it, when I don't even know where I'm coming from. Maybe I'm just a malcontent. Period, paragraph."

"Don't wallow. It doesn't become you. Give yourself a chance. And trust yourself! We perennial adolescents all go through this kind of thing once in a while. But seriously, Jill, I think something's happening. Stick with it."

"Yes, all right. Go with the flow, and all that."

"Jill?"

"Yes?"

"Remember to let go."

"Thanks, Chloe. I love you."

Jill sets the receiver down and thanks God for good friends. Then she sets out for the far side of the lake, only mildly conscious of the pull of the pink plane.

Once again, slipping into a canoe, she paddles toward the lake's center, allowing herself to drift physically and spiritually. This time she struggles less to actively find her centeredness, believing that if she lets it, it will come to her. She begins to have the feeling that if she can just stay here long enough, in this soothing and therapeutic place, she will find the quiet corner of her soul capable of releasing her from constraint and rationality. Out of the ritual of being rocked by the water her inner being would surface, she thinks, to float like a leaf on the lake. And from that presence would come new strength, fine energy, bold belief that would set her free once and for all.

In her reverie, she hardly hears the pink butterfly until its nose points directly toward her. It had seemed less urgent on this day to seek it. Still, it is pleasant to see her friend returning. The urgency appears now to be on the part of the plane. With precision and determination it bears down on her, and as it gets closer, Jill watches more intently, until sitting up, she is vaguely aware of a growing uneasiness. Is the noise of the engine erratic, more intense? Why does its usually languid motion suddenly seem so purposeful?

She watches it bear down on her, mesmerized, unable to move as it comes toward her with a precise lack of control. If it continues it will collide with her. But she makes no attempt to shift the canoe. What lies before her seems unchangeable. And with that thought, she transcends fear and waits with extraordinary calm, thinking, so this is what death is like!

Like a third party observer, she watches herself in the canoe watching the seaplane, and marvels at her own serenity. Nothing seems to matter. She feels a shedding of the heaviness which has enveloped her as only so much baggage. With an almost lightheaded sense of humor, she thinks, so this is the great Letting Go! And still the plane comes. And still in those eternal seconds she feels

free of fear, given over to the inevitable, part of some cos-
mic and loving force.

And now the plane zooms directly over her face as she
crouches in the canoe, breathing its hot, noisy breath on
her like a squawking pink flamingo barely able to flap its
wings into ascension. Then, with one final noisy asser-
tion, it is gone over the treetops, no trace of its terrible
tease save for the rocking of the canoe in its wake.

Gripping the sides of the canoe, Jill rises shaking to
her knees, and in response to the arrogance and intimi-
dation of the pink bird, shakes her fist mightily in the air,
shouting, "Bastard! You bastard!"

But with something quite different from rage, she rolls
her head back, and with a release so new to her that it
shakes her chest in great waves, she roars with laughter.
Only after a moment does she hear in her levity the great
heaving sobs wrenching forth from her throat. And then,
only then, does she realize that the sound of her own letting go resonates to the undulating lake, releasing a
reprise which rises up in the green mountains around
her like native Earth echoes.

MONA

✦ ✧ ✦

Home Is Where the Heart Is

Mona pulls the white sheers back from her kitchen window, raises the warm coffee cup to her lips, and peruses the sun peeking over the townhouses across from her apartment complex. It is a fine morning. How sad, she thinks, that it should be the worst day of my life.

Everything is as usual, she notes, and nothing will ever be the same. Joyce and Roger climb into their black Mazda and drive off to work. Sally stands by the school bus stop with Karen, smoothing her bangs to one side just as she does every morning. James, the building custodian, sweeps the front walk. She is grateful that none of them looks up toward her window. What will she do if they see her? Wave and smile? Jump behind the curtain? Burst into tears?

She turns to survey the large room adjacent to the kitchen. It is pleasant enough with its pale blue traditional sofa on which, opened up, she has slept every night, and its refinished bits and pieces of furniture. She looks at the desk and dining table and smiles to remember her elation the day she bid successfully for them at auction. That was nearly twelve years ago, when she had first set out on her own. What a sense of accomplishment once she'd finally sanded and then varnished the two pieces until they both looked like something to be proud of! Later she had added the four Shaker chairs to the dining table, and the two director's chairs which face the sofa with the trunk table in-between. Finally, plants and framed prints of Buffet and Mondrian had given the space an airy and eclectic decor.

Now it is all a clutter, cartons strewn expectantly around the room, labeled so that she knows precisely which box contains what. She picks her way across the one marked "Linens" and moves back toward the tiny kitchen to rinse her coffee cup. Suddenly it seems too long a journey to complete. She pauses at one of the chairs. Mustn't give in, she thinks, anxiety rising in her chest like a thunderstorm on the horizon. It will be all right. It *will* be all right!

Then the pride thing begins to take hold. She slips into the chair, crosses her blue-jeaned legs, and lets her head rest on the palm of her hand, her long gray hair falling over her arm. How had it come to this, she wonders again as she has done over and over this past month. It is too incredible, too awful, something that happens to other people.

It is, looked at with cool rationality, entirely explainable, she reminds herself. Nothing to be ashamed of, at least not in the sense that she is responsible for it. Her friends understand that, offer words of encouragement. She rises to continue her journey to the kitchen. Still, one can't take undue advantage. They have their own problems. And besides, who knows when the thing will end?

She folds her arms to wait for the kettle to boil again. It will be good to spend a little time with her sister, Kate. After all, something is bound to turn up, as Kate and her husband said. This is only a temporary setback. She's done so well on her own. Of course, there is no question of remaining with them for long. It will be hard enough on the twins sharing their room, and since the baby has come along, there isn't an ounce of extra space to be found at Kate's. Still, they have been kind enough to offer, and it would be rude not to stay with them for a little while.

The kettle whistles. Its shrillness makes her jump, setting off random word associations in her brain. Eviction, conviction, writ of restitution, stay of execution, destitution. Homeless, endless, wit's end, end of the line. How has it all run together, like the words?

She stirs the instant coffee and retreats slowly to the blue sofa, thinking back to her first days here. In the beginning, she'd been shaky, but it was okay. She hadn't wanted alimony, certain that with the settlement she could make a fresh start and then be entirely free of the man who had hurt her. After a while, when she got used to being alone, the freedom felt good, like the relief of getting over a bad stomachache. She liked being accountable to no one other than herself, enjoyed the new friends she was meeting at the community college, many of them women making new starts, like she was. Her job as a floor manager at Sloane's wasn't anything to shout about, but once she got her degree and some solid skills under her belt, she'd be able to give up sales and move on to something more interesting, more professional. Then the recession hit and she'd had to stop taking classes when her hours at work were reduced.

What time is it now anyway, she wonders. Surely the storage truck should have arrived. She rises and goes again to the window, staring at the curb.

Just the other day, on the front page of the paper, that awful picture had appeared. The one of the man being evicted from his home. How they'd gone on about his Doulton and silver, now heaped in pathetic piles on the reproduction Chippendale by the curb. God! The humiliation!

Surely the storage truck would come before the deadline. She'd been so emphatic about it.

Her boss had been emphatic too. "I'm sorry, Mona," he'd said. "I do appreciate the situation. But there's just nothing I can do about it. We're having to lay off hundreds. God knows, I could well be next." It was true enough. How could she be angry with him? Besides, no need to panic. She had some savings, and surely, someone willing to work could always find something.

But she hadn't. Scores of others lined up with her for every job she tried, and most of them were younger than she and, at least, could type.

"Look, it's bad times for everybody," Kate had said. "Why not put your stuff in storage and come stay with us for a while? It won't be for long."

She gets up from the sofa and walks, trancelike, to the dining table where the quilted heart-shaped pillow Kate gave her when she moved into the apartment lay. "Home Is Where the Heart Is," it says to her in rose-colored embroidery. She hugs it to her chest. Calm, she tells herself. Stay calm.

She looks at her watch. Where is that goddamn storage truck?

Still clutching the pillow, she moves to her desk and picks up the letter lying there with its two firm creases making the ends point up at her. "Dear Ms. Moorhead," it says. "We regret to inform you that owing to increased costs . . . " It was then she'd known she couldn't hang on any longer. A rent increase would eat through her remaining savings in two months. And then what? Would she eventually be found frozen to death in the doorway of some shop, like the bag lady on the news last winter who no longer had a face or an age or a life? It was too hideous to contemplate. That was when she'd made the decision to store her personal belongings and visit with Kate. Her remaining funds would go a lot further that way, and surely, surely, something would happen to bail her out of this mess.

She moves back to the window. The sun has shifted so that shadows are beginning to fall on the townhouses. The anxiety she always feels when the sun fades creeps into the hollow between her breasts. She shivers and wraps her cardigan around her. What if the truck doesn't come before her deadline to vacate? Will some burly men appear and bodily remove her and her belongings to the curb so that in the end the most humiliating thing of all will be to sit on her blue sofa by the street as the neighbors come home, one by one diverting their eyes and later saying to each other, Isn't it a shame about Mona?

She half smiles and an involuntary snort escapes from her throat. For a moment she thinks she might become hysterical.

She eyes the sofa. I'll just go and sit down and collect myself, she thinks. When it gets like this, I'm okay if I just start again. Breathe deeply, think clearly.

She waits for the pounding in her chest to stop. This must be when women in labor have to use those little brown bags so they don't pass out. I wonder what labor is really like, she thinks, her mind wandering in the way that it sometimes does when it can't bear any more thinking. She contemplates calling Kate, but realizes that the phone has been disconnected the day before. She begins to think about what would happen if she doesn't find a job in the next few weeks. She thinks about Hoover shanty towns and men jumping off of bridges and children with rickets in Ethiopia. In the back of her mind, the traces of a ridiculous song make their way into her consciousness. "I've got rhythm, who could ask for anything more?" Then she takes another deep breath and straightens the arch in her back until she is sitting upright as though she is about to give a speech. "It will be all right!" she announces emphatically, the sound of her own voice echoing back in the hollow of the stripped apartment.

But for now, where, Oh, Christ, where is that bloody storage truck?

FELICIA
✦ ✧ ✦
A Kind of Day

It's been the kind of day that makes people say "It's been one of those days!" when they grab a second beer or a stiff scotch. The kind of day that makes you feel tired and sad, glad when it's over so that you can start again. The kind of day that, when you were a child, always seemed to be gray and damp so that you wished for the smell of a hot iron pressing order back into life's chaos, or something cooking when you came home from school to reassure you that your mother would warm you with her smile and a snack. It was always a great sadness to me when my mother wasn't there to do that, which was often, because of her frequent incarcerations in the hospital for what was mysteriously referred to as her "problem." My father was no help. He was born tense and stayed tense all his life, which I think was part of my mother's "problem." Days like this one bring all those memories back to me, and I guess that's why I feel so lonely when they happen.

It started today with Matt being grouchy when he woke up. I always know when he's off color, or mad at me about something, because he makes coffee but doesn't pour any for me. I resent that. If he's angry, he ought to say so. Half the time, I never do find out what's eating him; he just gets over it and goes on. I resent that too. I always say what's on my mind. And I've never once poured my coffee and not his.

Sometimes I let it go, and sometimes I say, "What's wrong?"

"Nothing."

That really gets me.

"Nothing?"

"Nothing."

Then he leaves for work. I brood for a while, and then, depending if I'm premenstrual or not, I either slam a few cabinets or just let it be. Today I let it be.

At work, my boss, Marvella, snapped at me for everything and for nothing.

"I thought we might put the scarves on the display table like a rainbow fan," I suggested, to show I have initiative. (I work in Laurene's, a women's clothing shop, the smartest one in town.)

"Don't be silly!" she said. "That would be distracting."

Later on, I asked her where she wanted me to put the new shipment of cashmere sweaters.

"Why can't you decide what's best? That's what I pay you for!"

You can't win with her. If I use my own ideas, she says I'm being pushy. If I ask what she wants, she tells me I should use my own judgment once in a while. If I thought things would be any better anywhere else, I'd quit and find another job. But I've been around long enough to know that the devil you know is usually better than the one you don't. And God knows, I'll probably never get out of this town anyway, so I take what I can get and hope for the best.

Still, it doesn't hurt to be kind. My mother was the kindest person I ever knew and everyone loved her for it. Up until the day she died, she could get anyone to do anything for her, just because she was so nice to them. I think it really used to gall my father, because he couldn't stop himself being just a little bit mean, so people liked her a whole lot more than him. Even us kids.

Later in the day, on my break, I called up my friend Evelyn. She's got a really good job, secretary to one of the big lawyers in town, and she always cheers me up. Mary Rose, the receptionist, answered.

"Is Evelyn free?" I asked.

"She's swamped. Is this really important?" Mary Rose snarled at me, like she held the keys to the kingdom herself.

"Well, I guess I think it is or else I wouldn't be asking for her, would I?" I held my voice firm, but I felt like crying. Who did she think she was anyway to talk to me like that?

Evelyn came on the phone and told me not to worry. She made silly jokes about Marvella, and did a sort of Lily Tomlin take-off of her which was really pretty funny. I smiled, but I couldn't laugh because I still felt like crying. But I could tell she was busy, so I said I'd see her later and hung up. Then I went back to work and started making sure all the hangers were facing the same way and that the price tags weren't showing. Marvella never said a word to me the rest of the day, but when I was leaving she said, "I surely am glad you're working here. I don't know what I'd do without you!"

She's always doing things like that, which I can't figure out. Being mean one minute and nice the next. Once I went to a meeting at the women's center where a lady with beautiful gray hair and perfectly manicured red nails talked about "mixed messages" and "asserting yourself" with people who act nice but in a way that's mean. I think Marvella is doing the mixed message thing, but I haven't yet got to where I can do the asserting. That's why most of the time when Matt doesn't pour my coffee, I just let it go.

Anyway, after work I stopped at the 7-Eleven for milk and bread. The guy on duty, a greasy looking kid with pimples and an earring in one ear, was just plain rude when I asked if they had a *Ladies' Home Journal.*

"If it ain't there with them other magazines, we don't have it. We only got what's out there."

Well, it doesn't hurt to ask, does it?

The final straw was when the pickup truck hit me from behind at the corner of Warner and Broad. I mean, it wasn't as if the light turned red suddenly or anything. I slowed with the yellow, and stopped in good time. There was absolutely no reason for the man driving to hit me except that he wasn't watching where he was going. There wasn't any damage to his truck, that's for sure, and luckily, my car took it on the fender without a scratch. So what did he have to yell at me for?

"Christ, Lady! What the hell you doin'? Where'd you get your license, Sears? You oughtta learn how to drive that thing!"

I put my head on my hands, which were clinging to the top rim of the steering wheel, and began to cry. I guess he got scared then.

"You ain't hurt, are you?"

"No."

"Well then, what are you crying for?"

I didn't say anything at first. What's the use? But when he didn't go away, I said, "There has just been so much unkindness in this day. Is it really necessary for there to be so much unkindness?"

He looked at me like maybe I injured my head. And for some strange reason, I swear I don't know why, I said it again.

"Is it really necessary for there to be so much unkindness in the world?" This time I looked him straight in the eye.

He didn't know what to think. For a minute his eyes softened just a little, but it didn't last long. Then he took his Coors beer cap off, slapped it on his knee, and said, disgusted, "Women!" before climbing back into his truck. When the light turned green, we both drove on.

The tears were still coming down my face when I pulled into my driveway. I couldn't seem to stop crying once I started. Matt's car was already there. I wondered what kind of a mood he was in, but he was all smiles when I came into the kitchen.

"Hey, Babe, howya doin'?"

Then he saw that I wasn't right.

"What's the matter?"

I told him about my day, and about the jerk who hit me, and about how stupid he was when I asked him about people being kind. Matt put his arm around me.

"You on the rag?" he asked.

Now, isn't that just typical? If a guy's upset, he's not getting enough, and if a woman cries, she's got the curse. I swear!

"No, Matt," I said. "I am not on the rag. I just had one of those days."

"Every day is one of those days," he said, flipping on the TV before sinking into the sofa, a can of Bud in his hand.

Maybe. Maybe not. All I know right now is, I've got to call Evelyn. Because maybe if we could get together, have a few laughs about what happened, I might feel better. She's bound to understand.

She'll probably do a goofy bit about the guy in the truck first off. Then she'll go into the kitchen and in two minutes flat there'll be something special to eat. And in no time at all, I'll be feeling like tomorrow is going to be another story altogether.

I've always said Evelyn's a lot like my mom on a good day. Full of love, and as kind as the day is long.

SUSAN
✦ ✧ ✦
Six Ways to Sunday

It took me three weeks to draft the ad and another two to place it. If my friend Kurt hadn't kept after me, revising and rewriting, pushing me to call the paper and then to send the check, I probably never would have done it. It got to be a kind of thing between us, until finally it wore me down, although for weeks, it was the best part of going to the office. We got sillier and sillier, making up ridiculous ads that parodied those we read religiously.

"Aggressive, adorable Anglophile seeks companionship with bold, brassy Bavarian. Call ALPS-YES!"

"Born-again Christian looking for the ideal woman. If you relish the fine arts of home and hearth, and would love a brood to call your own, contact . . ."

"Divorced Spanish heiress wishes to meet humble *Homo sapiens* . . ."

Still, Kurt, who told me he'd met some really terrific dates through the singles column over the years, thought I was foolish not to try it.

"Hey Suz! What have you got to lose?" he'd ask. "Besides, how else does anyone meet anyone these days, especially under the circs?"

The "circs" are that I am newly divorced, depressed, and becoming increasingly reclusive. My job as a fundraiser for a group of homeless shelters doesn't exactly offer much in the way of opportunity for meeting people, and singles bars are definitely not my thing. Most of my friends are (miraculously) still married, and decidedly uneasy about fix-ups, and I don't blame them. The few times I've tried it have been unmitigated disasters.

So Kurt and I wrote the ad.

> SWF, creative, gregarious, warm, good sense of humor, seeks SWM for friendship and fun. If you like biking in the park, the Sunday *New York Times*, seafood fettucini, Placido Domingo, and serendipity, send particulars to Box 2939, *The Boston Globe*.

Four days after the ad ran, the first envelope arrived. After a week, an astounding ten responses had accumulated on my desk. I couldn't believe that there were so many SWMs loose in Boston when there were so many SWFs simultaneously moaning about the absence of bachelors in the very same city.

They were an odd assortment of fellows. I immediately discarded Fred, Adrian, and Jason, who all seemed slightly kinky in one way or another. (I mean, did I really want to meet a guy named Fred who has three Great Danes named Hansel, Gretel, and Miss Maud? Or Adrian, who currently lives in the basement of his father's house, but who plans to move once he liquidates his Leathers-and-Feathers shop? With Jason, the picture alone did it.)

I ruled out Daniel over the phone, when the woman who answered said she was his wife. So that left six of them, and I was only into the first week of this gig.

Last Monday, I met Charlie for coffee. His bio sounded interesting enough. After all, someone who collects seashells can't be all bad. We met, at his suggestion, at a diner called The Cabbie, just outside Brookline. It took me a while to catch on. It wasn't until Charlie told me, somewhat sheepishly, that he drives a Yellow Cab that I realized why there were so many cabs parked outside.

"I hope you don't mind," he said apologetically. "I'm just doing it until I can get back into sales. The recession really hit me hard." His resume had said that he sold software.

"No," I said, lying through my teeth. I had often wondered, hypothetically, whether I would have the courage to fall in love with a Ph.D. cab driver who had chosen the free life, but I had decided I couldn't. I am a snob.

But that isn't what turned me off of Charlie. What turned me off of Charlie was Shelley.

Shelley was the student Charlie insisted on telling me about, the one he had met at The Cabbie last year. We'd been talking about the ad, and how hard it is to meet people.

"Sometimes, though, they just fall into your lap!" Charlie said with a loud and decidedly locker room chuckle. "Like Shelley."

Shelley, it seems, had been hard up for a buck during her junior year at Simmons, so she had offered herself to Charlie over a friendly cup of coffee at The Cabbie.

"I've never done this before," she told Charlie. "I mean, I wouldn't want you to get the wrong idea or anything. I'm just a little hard up for cash this month, and, well . . . if you want to spend the night with me . . . it'll cost you."

"So what was I gonna do?" Charlie asked me, as if there were absolutely no alternatives. "I mean, a gorgeous young thing throws herself at me. Who am I to look a gift horse in the mouth?"

I stared at him, knowing that there would be more.

"And you know, it was amazing! I really got it off with that kid. I mean, she was something else in bed! And . . . " Charlie stopped then, and looked at me like I was a nun.

"But my God, what am I doing telling you all this, huh? I got carried away here. It was a one-time thing. Not like I'm that kind of guy or anything. Know what I mean?"

"Yeah. Actually, Charlie, I do. More than you know, I know what you mean. It's been real."

I threw a dollar bill on the table, grabbed my coat off the hook by the booth, and said, "See you around."

On Tuesday, I went to Hank's place for a drink. This seemed an entirely reasonable and safe thing to do after the hour plus we'd spent on the phone a few days earlier. He had intrigued me, I had to admit, beginning with his deep and resonant voice. I had visions of a kind of Kenny Rogers-cum-Mark Rothko. Hank is an abstract artist who moonlights full-time as a graphics specialist for an ad agency.

He did kind of look like Kenny Rogers, with his gray hair and salt-and-pepper beard, his twinkly blue eyes, and his barrel chest. But it wasn't his physical appearance that caught my eye when I entered his apartment. It was the decor. Not the mirrors, really. The hearts.

Hank's apartment was a veritable tunnel of love. I entered, having gone carefully down the stairs to his "lower level" pad, to find hearts of every shape and size (but not every color; just red) dangling from the ceiling in a raucous montage of romance. There seemed to be millions of them because of the mirrors on the walls, reflecting the mad array of crimson as if it were February 14th and Hank were Cupid personified.

"Now don't get the wrong idea," Hank said as soon as my eyes fixed on the heart above my head as I came through the front door.

"No! Wouldn't think of it!" I said. The smell of incense nearly choked me into silence.

"It's just a thing I have. I love hearts and flowers and candles and incense burning! I was kind of hoping you liked those things too."

"Well, I do, Hank, but . . . "

"You just come on over here and have a seat on the couch. I'll pour us some wine and we'll talk. I promise. There's nothing more to it than that."

That was fair enough. And honest. We spent the evening sipping chilled Chablis and talking and it was all very interesting, especially the part about how, when you got right down to it, Hank was still crazy about his ex-wife and hoped to somehow woo her back.

At l0:30 I thanked him, wished him luck, and hurried home to catch the news.

On Wednesday, I had the night off. Kurt, who kept tabs on me anyway, but especially now that my dance card was full, called from Philadelphia, where he'd gone on business, to see how I was holding up.

"How you doing?" he asked, hopefully.

"Swell, Kurt. Just swell."

"Are we having fun yet?"

"Well, I wouldn't exactly say fun. But it's been interesting." I proceeded to tell him about Charlie/Shelley, and Hank and the hearts.

"Whoa," he said. Hank only said "Whoa" when he was speechless. "Well, so you had a couple of unusual events. So what! Nothing ventured, nothing gained! Hang in there. What's next?"

"Next is tomorrow night with Sven. Drinks at The Ritz, no less."

"No kidding! That sounds promising!"

"Yeah," I said. "Stay tuned."

"Okay. See you next week. I'll be dying for the next installment!"

For Sven and The Ritz, I wore leather boots draped by a black skirt, a wool shawl over an ecru turtleneck, and my broad-brimmed black hat. (I was beginning to enjoy getting into character for my little tête-à-têtes.) It was definitely a smart move. Sven, a Norwegian businessman who crossed the Atlantic as if it were the Charles River, greeted me in his pin-striped suit and paisley cravat by standing and kissing my hand.

"Mademoiselle," he said, facetiously I thought, but I wasn't sure. His smile was warm.

"What may I order for you?" he asked, the epitome of gallant.

I smiled and said to the space between Sven and the waiter, "Chardonnay, please." (I wanted Sven to know that I could take care of myself.)

"And an assortment of hors d'oeuvres," Sven added. (Touché.)

"Well, tell me all about yourself," Sven said. "I found your ad charming."

The ritual exchange of autobiographies got us through two glasses of wine and the tray of smoked salmon and caviar delicately plunked onto designer crackers. I embellished my life and times only to the extent necessary to make my persona match my outfit, and Sven told the truth, I'm sure. Why else would he have explained our little soiree as one of the "diversions" he enjoyed when he was in America? He hoped I wasn't offended. Indeed, he'd very much like to see me next time he was in town. Dinner, perhaps?

I wanted to say, with all the glamour I could muster, "Gee, Sven, that would be swell," just so that I could do a replay for Kurt, but I knew I'd never carry it off. So I just said, "That would be nice."

When I got home, I added Sven to my growing "Reject" file, where he seemed in odd, but curiously deserved company with Charlie and Hank. Onward and upward, I thought, contemplating Friday night with Jerome, whom I desperately hoped would invite me to call him Jerry.

Jerry — I never waited to be invited, I just called him that straight away and he didn't protest — made the week seem brighter right away. He was reasonably good-looking, and very funny. He told great stories and jokes, one after another, in perfect dialect all through our dinner of pasta pesto (at least he remembered that I like Italian food) and then over cappuccino, he grew suddenly serious.

"I can't keep this up," he said, suddenly mournful.

"Excuse me?" I felt as if my esophagus was a silo for parmesan cheese.

"I've tried. I have really tried. But I'm going to level with you because I like you." I didn't know how he could know that since he had been doing all of the talking, but it was a nice compliment. I always like to be trusted.

"I'm gay."

I steadied myself by putting my wrists firmly against the checkered tablecloth, fork in one hand, spoon in the other, and smiled at him affirmatively, hoping desperately that my demeanor conveyed acceptance.

"That's okay with me, Jer," I said, feeling a new intimacy inspired by his sharing. "But why in the world did you answer my ad?"

"I did it for my mother," he said. "Understand?"

Oddly enough, I understood perfectly.

"But I just can't keep this up. I'm going to have to come out. Telling her is just so hard."

Then he talked a lot about his life, his mom and dad, his public life, his secrets. I liked him enormously. I hope he believed me when I said, sometime after one in the morning, that I wanted to be friends. He said he did.

"I'm going to call you next week," I said, when he dropped me at my front door. "Just to see how you're doing."

"That'd be great." Then he kissed me on the cheek and walked away, his head down. At the corner, he squared his shoulders, tightened the belt on his trenchcoat, and lifted his head.

Call Jerome, I wrote on my calendar.

It's Saturday now and I'm exhausted, but there's still Victor to go. Victor, in many respects, seems the most promising. According to his bio, Victor is a biochemist with a penchant for Janis Joplin, Scott Joplin, French wine, Italian food, Japanese prints, and all things English. He has so many interests it's almost frightening, but he sounded like a regular guy on the phone and I liked the way he invited me to talk too. The only thing I wondered about was when he said he doesn't "do elevators" and could we meet in front of the Cafe Florian so that we could go downstairs together. It should be a pretty interesting evening.

Then, tomorrow, in between cleaning the bathroom and doing my laundry, I'll go through the new envelopes in my "Consider" file. I'll have to. Kurt will want to know just how things stand for next week when he gets back to the office on Monday.

Gosh, come to think of it, it'll be good to see Kurt again.

NATALIE
♦ ◇ ♦

A Heart of Gold

The idea first came to me when I was sitting on the john. I'd been in the bathroom a long time, pretending I had stomach cramps so I could have some time to myself. The motel room had begun to give me claustrophobia with its solitary window obscured by cheap print curtains and its spotted orange-brown carpet curling slightly at the bathroom door. Maybe it wouldn't have seemed so small and dingy if it hadn't been pissing rain outside. That was the problem with the Pacific Northwest. When it was good, it was very good, but a large part of the time it was just plain awful. "You know what they say," someone from Seattle told me when I'd first moved out. "When you can't see the mountains, it's raining. When you can, it's going to rain!"

We'd arrived the night before and it was raining then. Torrential blobs hit us on the head and dove down the backs of our necks as we transferred our respective weekend bags from my car to the room. The rain cast a pall over an already darkened weekend, one that I knew I should have aborted before it began. But when it came to Pierre Claude, I never could say no.

Our relationship had spanned four years, two continents, and the fifteen-year gap in our ages. Fate was always throwing us together. From that first chance meeting in Paris at the Louvre when I was a starry-eyed student to my overseas gig at the American Hospital to his foreign jaunts to deliver papers at medical conventions, every time I thought I'd seen the last of him, there he was again at my doorstep assuming I would be at the ready. The trouble was, I was. I've never been given much to excesses, being the product of a Depression family, but among them (in addition to putting too much peanut butter on my bread and using a fresh Brillo pad each time) is being too available too often to Mr. Wrong.

Pierre was the ultimate Mr. Wrong. Charming, multifaceted, intensely interested in all sorts of esoteric things (he collected miniatures, stamps, coins, and travel brochures), intelligent, debonair, full of savoir faire. So much savoir that you never realized how unfair he was being until it was too late. It wasn't until he'd broken my heart into a million fragments that I understood what a taker he was, how he had sucked the life out of me while I felt certain that if only I hadn't been so demanding, things might have been different.

So how could I possibly find myself, yet again, in a motel room with him? Like I said, I never could say no to Pierre Claude.

When he wrote to say he'd be in San Francisco and how about a weekend together for old time's sake, I hesitated. Enough, I thought. This has got to stop so that I can get on with my life. By the time I sat down to pen an answer, I had weakened. Seattle had been lonely. My work at the lab was stimulating, and I was definitely getting my life back in order, but socially it was a desert. And to be blunt, I was horny. So I conned myself that I could handle just one more weekend. I agreed that he could come up from the Bay. We would drive down to the Oregon coast and he could leave from Portland. That way, I'd stay in control.

Fat chance. Before Saturday was over, I had the distinct feeling that my psyche was doing a slow fade, like the Wicked Witch of the West who finally dissolved into vapors so that she could no longer threaten Dorothy. I'd started out feeling like a truant child. But I graduated into grade A sucker after lunch. That's when Pierre, who'd told me over Bloody Marys and grilled cheese sandwiches about the new love of his life (Ellen), asked if I would mind helping him pick out a nice souvenir for her. I wanted to vomit. In his lap. Instead, I smiled, ordered another Bloody, and said, "Don't you think that's a bit much, really?"

"Darling!" he said. "You have such exquisite taste."

Pierre is the only man who's ever called me Darling. It used to send shivers up me, like I was the only one who ever got called that, except for royalty. It still had an effect. My comment, however, seemed to have none on him. He actually wasn't capable of seeing how ludicrous his request was. Ellen was Ellen, and I was me, and we both knew about each other, and fit into entirely different compartments of his life, and that was that. Simple. Clean. Cruel. I wondered how long Ellen would last.

But the bitch is, I did it. Off we went to a cozy little craft and jewelry shop called The Button Hole, which seemed to specialize not in buttons at all, but in butterflies, flowers, and hearts. I spotted a lovely handmade silver and onyx pendant that I would have loved. But Ellen? How was I to know. What kind of a woman was she, I wondered. Was she a sweet young thing who had yet to figure Pierre out? Or a shrew who was just in it for good sex? Or just too lonely to care? It didn't matter. Pierre, I suspected, would consider the piece too expensive. "Ouch!" he said when I showed it to him. I know my man. My next suggestion was a gold-filled abstract heart hung on a chain. The fact that its center was hollow did not escape me, and for a moment, I imagined that some day it would represent a symbolic bond between me and the unknown Ellen. I nearly laughed out loud at the thought. Pierre saw me grinning and said, "Well, if you like it that much, it must be the thing." Fleetingly, I wondered if he would think to get me a trinket, sort of an interest payment, but of course, he didn't. He'd given me a book about Paris when he'd arrived, a sort of high-gloss photojournalism book, the kind you get for $4.98 on a good day at Crown Books. That, and the weekend, was to be my "beni."

Mission accomplished, we set off further down the coast, ominous clouds hovering over us like a sign from God the closer we got to the ocean. We stopped in a few places, to putter, walk, have a cup of chocolate, chit-chatting as if we were a regular number off to have a sexy weekend together. I felt pretty low most of the time and even had fleeting fantasies of confrontation, but then decided to leave it alone and accept the fact that without this weekend, I never would have been able to come to full closure on Pierre Claude.

Besides, in the purely physical sense, the man still got to me. He made love like no one else I'd ever been with and I wanted to experience it again, just one last time. It had been a long, lean season.

Toward evening, we found the motel. It wasn't much to look at, but it had, to commend it, a fabulous view of the ocean. By walking just a few feet away from the front door of our room, we could take in a panoramic sweep of coastal rock, creviced inlets below, and the violent, angry waves of the storm. In spite of the rain, we stood there after we'd checked in, like a latter-day Cathy and Heathcliff whose passion has dissipated along with their inelegant change of costume to reflect twentieth-century reality. After a less-than-noteworthy meal of steak and a bottle of burgundy at a local restaurant, we settled in for sex. It was a routine familiar to us from the days when we first went at it like a clandestine Abelard and Heloise. And as always, it was stunning. Sex as sex was meant to be. Long. Slow. Titillating. Tender. Exquisite. When Pierre Claude and I made love, mountains moved, the earth shook, and all the metaphors of Avon romance novels took on new meaning. We also remembered what it was like when we were truly in love. And in that long brief night, it was possible once again to care for each other.

The morning was another story. When the light penetrated the flimsy curtains and woke us, I had a stale taste in my mouth and a strong case of morning-after regrets.

That was nothing to what I felt a few minutes later when Pierre got up, threw on a robe, went to the desk, and started writing.

"Ellen," he smiled by way of explanation.

I felt like a whore, and pulled the covers up around my neck. That was when I got up, wrapped a blanket around me, and went to the john. After a while, Pierre called out, "Are you all right?"

I didn't answer. Just sort of groaned, which was honest enough. Eventually I gave up the throne. Then I got dressed and peered out the window. The rain had slowed to a drizzle. I put on my raincoat and walked out to the edge of the cliff. The air was sharp and I felt desolate. I couldn't get the idea I'd thought of in the john out of my mind. At first, it was only a comic fantasy. But it had begun to take hold, and I actually found myself plotting the details. It would be dead easy. And divine retribution. At what point does an idea become an obsession, something we know, against all other judgment, we will, we must, do? I don't know exactly when that moment came for me, but sometime between walking out, sitting on a huge boulder looking at the sea, and returning to the room, I had crossed the line.

When I came back, he was still writing. Chalk one up for Ellen. She inspired longer love letters than I had ever done. He smiled at me again. I wasn't sure if his face really seemed contorted, or if I was projecting the look I was certain crossed my own face. "Be ready in a jiffy," he said, full of energy and good cheer. His French accent made the expression sound silly.

"Great," I managed.

Then he went into the bathroom to shave and shower. Effortlessly, as if I were floating on air, I collected my things, put them haphazardly into my bag, wrote off my toiletry items which were still in the bathroom, glanced around the room, and slung my purse over my shoulder, car keys in hand. In one final, spontaneous, brilliant coup, I also grabbed both pairs of Pierre's trousers.

Driving north on Interstate 5, I suddenly got a fierce case of the giggles. The thought of him standing there, literally with his pants down, in the middle of Oregon somewhere, with no way out, made me howl. I nearly peed myself. My stomach hurt. Then the sun broke through the proverbial silver lining etching one mother of a cloud in the sky ahead of me. I turned the radio on full blast, rolled down my window, stuck my elbow out, and said to no one in particular, "ALL RIGHT! I'm on the road again!"

SARA

✦ ✧ ✦

The Shrink

I couldn't put my finger on it at first, but I was sure I knew the guy. I watched him walking toward me in the hospital corridor and something in his step, the tentative way he moved from one foot to the other as though he were avoiding puddles of quicksand, was familiar. But it wasn't until he was practically on top of me that it clicked.

"Dr. Arnstein!" He stared blankly at me.

"Sara. Sara Jacoby. You . . . "

"Oh, yes! Yes! I do remember you." He continued to gaze at me in a fog, his dense glasses sliding down his narrow nose so that he bore an incredible likeness to a myopic sparrow. The funny thing was, I didn't remember him being so diminutive and so ridiculous looking. Had he always been so scrawny? So emaciated? Had his hair always stood out as if he'd just touched an electric socket with wet hands? Of course, fourteen years is a long time, I reasoned. It would be easy to forget. Some things, that is.

"Sara Jacoby!" he spouted suddenly, con gusto. He had obviously just gotten it. Just in case, though, I thought I'd refresh his memory.

"Yes. You were my psychiatrist fourteen years ago, remember? You were the one who decided I needed a week of rest. But it was twelve weeks, wasn't it? Twelve weeks, and lots of lithium and God knows what else, before you let me out. Do you remember now?"

"It will only be for a week, Mrs. Jacoby. You could use a rest. Everyone thinks it's best."

"And who's everyone?"

"Why, Dr. Arnstein. And your husband, of course."

"Why doesn't anyone want to know what I think?"

"Well, dear, you're not really in any condition to decide, are you?"

"I don't know. Maybe not. But things seem a little out of control here. I thought I was just coming into the hospital to find out why I have such headaches, and now you say I'm going to the Psych Unit. I don't understand what's happening here."

"Apparently, the doctor thinks your headaches may be psychosomatic."

"You mean he thinks I'm crazy? Making it up? What?"

"No, dear. Not at all. You're probably just tired. After all, why else would someone like you be so despondent? You're such an attractive woman, and my, that nice husband, and those lovely children!"

"Well, well, well! My! My! How are you, Sara? I must say you're looking fine. Just fine!"

His eyes were beginning to focus. They seemed sad to me, like the black tiles in those endless mosaic ashtrays I'd made in the hospital all those years ago. I also noticed that he called me Sara.

"What brings you here anyway?" he asked, cautiously.

"Oh, I'm just visiting someone," I said. He seemed visibly relieved.

"You still call patients by their first names, I see." I smiled, looking straight into his mosaic eyes.

He lowered his lids and looked at his feet for so long I thought he might have died and forgotten to fall over. Then he said, "You know, that is the one thing I remember about you. After your hospitalization, you came to the office and you said something about wanting to call me by my first name."

"That's right. I wanted to know why you could call me Sara and I still had to call you Dr. Arnstein. It didn't seem fair."

He laughed and brushed his hand across his lips.

"You never came back after that."

"No. I never did."

"Well, you seem to be just fine."

"I am just fine."

"You know, now I let my patients call me whatever they want to."

"That's nice." I had the feeling I was supposed to reward him for good behavior.

"It's good for business." He laughed. I guess he was making a joke.

"You know all that stuff about my mother and my father and my subconscious? All that was garbage. You know that, don't you?"

He looked at me then as if I had just shot him in the foot. His forehead tightened as if he were in pain and then he pursed his lips and squinted his eyes so that he looked even more like a wounded sparrow. I had a sudden impulse to feed him through an eyedropper so that he would revive.

"The problem was really that I was in a very bad marriage. A very destructive marriage," I said.

"I asked you about your marriage," he said defensively.

"You asked me about my sex life. Different thing."

He looked at his watch. For a moment, I had a terrible temptation to restrain him, to torture him with post-mortem insight, to force-feed him Feminism 101, to make him write 1,000 times, "Sisterhood is powerful" until, sweating and shaking, he pleaded for relief. Instead, I said, "Do you know what changed my life?"

He shook his head like a repentant child.

"A story. It's called 'The Yellow Wallpaper.' A woman wrote it and it saved her life too."

I don't think he'd ever heard of Charlotte Perkins Gilman, or of her autobiographical tale of madness. I also doubted that he would run out to buy a copy. But maybe he liked the story as I told it to him.

The irony of it, I thought, watching him walk down the corridor a few minutes later, was that I'd held him captive for twelve minutes. He'd kept me prisoner for twelve weeks. But somehow, it didn't seem to matter. Instead, it was suddenly ridiculous that he should have had so much power over my life. Ludicrous that I should have believed everything he said. Wildly unimaginable that this ineffectual, pathetic character had influenced me in any way.

A week later I sent him a copy of *The Yellow Wallpaper and Other Stories,* inscribed "To Jack, Hope this is helpful, Sara." I don't really expect an acknowledgment. But I sure hope the guy reads it. Like they say, "a change is as good as a rest," and judging from the way he looked last week, poor Jack Arnstein could use a bit of both.

JUDITH

✦ ✧ ✦

Flashbacks

✦ I ✦

Tall and erect, with salt-and-pepper hair growing erratically toward dark, deep-set eyes. Tweedy and unkempt, attractive in an Englishman. Moving from one gallery to the next, she knew his appreciation of art was overpowered only by curiosity about herself, a young woman in a red raincoat. Later, while sipping Amontillado sherry together at the Chandos Bar off Trafalgar Square, he confessed. "It was the raincoat. And that you were alone. That's why I never took you for American!"

"I suppose you think all American women have long blonde hair, California tans, and London Fogs?" she teased. "And travel in droves."

"Something like that."

Easy talk. Real talk. Past the preliminaries, and still a hint of secrets kept. Rain pellets on the window making the Chandos nook with its chintz bench cushions and brass rubbings feel like home. Sherry warming the body.

"I wish I could take you to dinner, but I've got a plane to catch back up north."

"Never mind. I'll walk you to the tube."

The hint of moisture in the air hovering like thin fog after a rain. Arms touching as long strides make up for lost minutes. Past the Cavell monument, across the wet square, to Charing Cross station. Then, a kiss, a glance that makes talking moot, and, like a scene from a World War II movie, he disappears into the bowels of British Rail. A curious rending, and in three hours, all of life has changed.

✦ II ✦

"Checking out today, then?"

"Yes. I'm going on to Paris."

"Well, you'll need a good breakfast. Oh, I nearly forgot. There's a letter for you." The plump Italian woman hands over an envelope and, smiling, hurries off to the kitchen while her dour English husband scowls over his accounts. The small dining room with its flowered wallpaper and white embroidered tablecloths begins to fill up with tourists seduced from their rooms by the smell of fried bacon and eggs. It is a pleasant enough bed and breakfast.

"The Queen's Court, 182 Inverness Rd., Bayswater, London." The handwriting is an unfamiliar graceful scrawl, the postmark York. Whoever . . . and then inaudibly, Oh! She opens the blue envelope with a peculiar sensation in her stomach.

"It's never happened to me before, please believe that. Meeting you has done something quite extraordinary. I can't stop thinking of you. So there are things I must tell you . . . "

Why does the wife matter? It's not really a surprise, not even that it's a poor marriage. One could have easily guessed — the loose references to "we," the office address instead of home. They'll never meet again. It was just an infatuation, something to make a first European journey more memorable. Funny, the sense of loss . . . Still, a reply is in order. Acknowledgment. Closure.

And so the correspondence is begun.

✦ III ✦

It goes on for nearly a year, until the letters become central to their lives. Through the written word, they grow intimate. "My dearest darling," his letters begin. She attempts restraint. "Dearest Derek." There is something unnatural in the deepening knowledge of each other across the sea, without touch or sight; this wants watching. But she hungers for the letters, devours them when they come, begins to plan her return. He encourages her, longingly and passionately, even as he reminds her that under the circumstances, the decision must be hers. She makes it freely, she says, to live abroad, as she has always wanted to do. He is the catalyst, not the cause, she tells him, embracing the delusion almost as much as he does, and in the spring, she is on a ship carrying her eastward on a sea swelling with possibility.

✦ IV ✦

He comes aboard to greet her and the sight of him catches her breath. He is taller, older, nattier than she remembered. She knows that tonight she will sleep with him, and he is suddenly a stranger. What have I done? she thinks. Why am I here? But then his arms are around her, his breath warm on her neck, his long, lean body fitting against her own slenderness as if it were meant to be there and the year and the sea and the questions between them dissolve and nothing matters but their togetherness, no matter what it will cost them. As they leave the ship, the purser calls after her, "Hello, Miss! Letter for you. Just brought on board. You nearly missed it!" On the envelope the now familiar script that has become her lifeline. They laugh, and he kisses her full and warm and long on the mouth. "Never mind about that now!" he says, grinning broadly, and leads her to his car, and a two-week holiday in the villages of Cornwall, so idyllic, so loving, that she can have no idea of the price to be paid.

They lie side by side in the inn at Dorchester and watch through a skylight dormer as daylight intrudes. Their lovemaking has been good; full and rich and kind.

They are deeply satisfied. She nestles into the side of his long body, warm and welcoming, and he strokes her face. "Imagine," she says with the hint of a giggle. "Five o'clock in the morning and we're actually talking to each other. I can't believe it won't take five days to know what you're thinking!"

"You'll always know what I'm thinking, my darling."

And on this, their first morning, she has no reason to wonder.

The days in Cornwall are languid, abundant with English treasures. They awake lazily, make love in a room full of seaside sounds and smells. Crisp white window curtains flap in the breeze like sheets hung out to dry. The chill of salt air makes them huddle together, and only the smell of breakfast and appetites made ravenous by heightened senses force them from their nest. After breakfast, they stroll to the quayside to watch the fishing boats bobbing like colorful corks in the harbor, then up the hill to the stone church and on to the village center.

After lunch they visit neighboring villages, one more beautiful than the next in their Lilliputian settings. In Mevighessey they eat cockles and mussels fresh from the sea; in Lerryn they sip bitter in the pub while a group of men, local bellringers, sing a cappella "Little Jimmy Brown," and it is so beautiful she cannot keep from weeping. "Why are you crying?" he asks. "Because I'm so happy, and the rest of the world is so sad," she says.

In the evening they cross from Polruan to Fowey on the foot ferry to visit the pubs and listen to ballads in Gaelic and old English. She is a novelty, this American in the red raincoat, and he smiles as the locals ask what brought her there. They play darts and dance if there's music and, on one special night, the pub even stays open past last call, and the foot ferry must wait to carry them back to their room in the inn. In the morning, the seagulls squawk and carry on like angry chaperons and they laugh and make love and miss breakfast.

One day they go to Devon, near the moors, to meet an old army buddy in The King George. The huge fireplace welcomes them against the chill of an afternoon rain. After a while, fire and friendship warm them. He is called Tom, his wife Diana. They are good people and never ask how it came to be that they are there together. It feels good to have friends. "I hope we see you again," she says. Diana smiles. Afterward, he tells her, "Tom told me, in the men's room, how lucky I was to have you. Things aren't going very well between him and Diana."

And then, as they knew it must, the holiday ends and they drive back to London together. He drops her at the Queen's Court, where she will stay once more until she can find a flat and begin her new job. She tries desperately to be cheerful, not to weep at the parting. She has promised herself never, ever to ask more of him than he has offered to give. Still, his farewell seems a bit cavalier. "Bye, bye, Darling! See you in a few weeks. Cheerio!"

◆ V ◆

The first weeks are lonely. She is busied with moving to the West End flat she has found to share with two other professional women, and with starting her new job in marketing for the accounting group she left in New York, but mostly she thinks about him, wonders what he is doing in the evenings, why he can't manage to call. It would be difficult, of course, from home. Still, he often goes to the office to write her long, flourishing letters. "I long for you. You are my only happiness. I cannot imagine life without you anymore." After a while, the letter she has most wanted to see comes. "I will be in London next month! We can have a long weekend away. I count the days!"

She also counts, and by the time he arrives, she is trembling with anticipation. They set off late on a Friday evening for Coventry, Banbury, and Warwick Castle, hungry for all that can be packed into the three days granted them by his business travel. Neither is disappointed. The English countryside is Constable unfrozen from the canvas, they are Barrett and Browning come to life. Their time together is so exquisitely pleasurable that it becomes nearly painful, and when the time comes for parting, she feels her soul shrunken as if it had been seared by a branding iron. He too is sad, but his equilibrium seems curiously untouched. So unlike a woman, she thinks.

And so the pattern is established. Every month or six weeks, a rendezvous. Vivid, extraordinary moments stretched out and packed into three days in the Midlands, or Salisbury, or Cambridge, or Canterbury. Once he even meets her in York, taking her on a pub crawl dangerously close to home, showing her off to the few friends who have his confidence about his "American girlfriend." And always it is the same. Passionate, rich, and full, with melancholy intruding as gatekeeper when their time is up. Once they fly to the west coast of Ireland where he (and his wife) owns a cottage by the sea. He makes love to her in the bed where his wife still sleeps when she is there. Afterward, she opens a drawer and finds a woman's sweater and she feels ashamed. "I don't want to come here again," she says. He touches her arm. "Don't be silly, Darling!" he says. "She hasn't been here with me in two years."

Once, on one of their weekends, he seems distant, preoccupied. She watches him climb a heather-covered hill and stand, a solitary figure, on a precipitous cliff at the top. She feels frightened, not only of what would happen if he fell, but beyond that. Fear grips her stomach and chest in a way she does not understand and she wants to shout at him "Come down! Come down!" but her voice is frozen within her, and she knows that he would not come anyway. He turns and waves at her and even though she cannot see his face, she knows that he is grinning.

Later, in the night, he turns from her, pulling her toward him from behind. "Don't ever leave me," he pleads suddenly. "Promise me you won't ever leave me." "I won't leave you," she says, putting the blankets around him, despite her own chill, because giving is in her nature. And because taking is in his, he pulls the blanket's warmth, and hers, around him, and sinks into sleep.

The weeks that pass now between their times together grow more difficult for her. Their weekends become respite for the long lean days and nights without him, when life seems shallow and unconnected to reality. She tries to immerse herself in all that London can offer, but it is empty. Quietly, she craves her old job, where she was excited far above what the new workplace allows. And she wonders why it seems so easy for him. For the first time, she begins to ponder the future, and questions till now repressed break through her consciousness. And of these, the loudest is When?

One day Tom comes to London and rings her for lunch. They meet at the pub closest to her office. "It's wonderful to see you!" he says, like an old and dear friend. "And you! I really enjoyed that day in Devon. How's Diana?" "Oh, you know, it's lonely down there. She isn't very happy, really. It's not like you and Derek. God, it must be wonderful to be that much in love!" She smiles, sad for him, and for Diana, and for herself.

"Why not bring her to London," she offers. "Maybe the four of us could have a weekend." But she knows they never will.

Soon after, she calls Derek, who is coming in two weeks. "I saw Tom," she says. "We had lunch. I'm so sorry about him and Diana." A long pause. "Yes, well, there you are. Anyway, I'll be there Friday week. God, I'm longing to see you." On the Friday he is due, she waits from eleven o'clock in the morning to hear that he has arrived, but the call doesn't come until just before five. "Where've you been? I've been worried!" "I got in late. I'll meet you at the office at half five." She hears the tension in his voice and feels a paralyzing chill creep up her stomach to her chest. She sees it in his face when she races down to the lobby, wild with longing, to meet him. They go to the pub, the same one where she and Tom had lunch, and order drinks. "I've been dying to see you," she says, taking his hand. "What's wrong?" "How long have you been sleeping with Tom?" he asks, his black eyes flashing rage at her like a demented stranger.

She wants to scream. To throw beer in his face. To run for her life across the road into the park until gasping for breath she can cling to a tree for support. She wants him to follow and she wants to claw his eyes out. But instead, frozen to the seat, she hears the sound of her own sobbing, and realizes that her chest is heaving and she cannot breathe.

"Let's get out of here," he says, leading her past the tables of staring patrons, some of whom know her from the office. In a trance, she reaches the hotel they have booked, her mind racing and stumbling as if being chased by a wild herd. "How could you say that? How could you think it?" she hears herself say over and over again. "Don't you realize what a good friend Tom is? Don't you know how much I love you? Have you got any idea how much he envies you?" And all the while that the stunned questions spill out of her, a piece of her rages quietly within, so deep, so untapped that it is almost imperceptible, overpowered by a curious sense of calm which has begun to settle over her like exhaustion.

"I'm sorry, oh my God, I'm sorry," he pleads like a lost child. "I love you. I love you so much I go mad sometimes. I began to imagine all sorts of things when you told me you'd seen him. Christ, I'm so sorry. I must be crazy. Please, please, forgive me." He smothers her with kisses, wiping her eyes, pushing her hair out of her face. They collapse on the bed and hold each other as if it were a fragile sailboat in a squall, and as dusk overtakes them, she falls into the fitful sleep of a feverish child. When she awakes, he is sitting in the chair watching her. He smiles tentatively. As she begins to rise, a fly buzzes past her face, and she sees for the first time that the hotel room they are in is shabbily lit, and slightly sordid.

✦ VI ✦

"I don't feel I can go on like this much longer," she finally tells him on one of their London weekends. (They are less inclined to go to the countryside now, as if they had run out of places, and fantasies.) It's not just us. It's my work. My life. Where's it all going?" "You knew what the situation was when you came," he says. "It was your choice. I never asked you. I never said I would want to marry again. I'm not cut out for it. There were no conditions for either of us. We just wanted to be together. Besides, you said you were coming for lots of other reasons." In the end she knows it is futile to discuss it and slowly, slowly, she lets the knowledge of what she must do wash over her. When she is certain, she says, "I'm leaving. There's nothing else to be done. I must leave." "Perhaps it would be best," he says.

✦ VII ✦

Years later, when she could think about it sanely, rationally, and truly understand him, and herself, she saw that she had had in her an instinct for emotional survival so strong that it enabled her to go. But at the time, it was the weakness that precedes death that allowed her to go through the necessary motions of leaving. And all through the packing and leave-taking, still they made love as starving people cling to scraps of sustenance, and took from their days all that could be drawn from them. And even in the last moment, because, she supposed, none of it had ever seemed real, she went through the

motions with dignity and grace, and only later, much
later, when they sealed the airplane door like the lid of a
coffin, did she let go and give way to a grief so deep, so
wrenching, so pervasive, that she felt, even months and
years later, as though every organ of thinking, and feeling, and being in her body had been surgically excised.

✦ VIII ✦

Afterward, there were a few letters at first, then
Christmas cards. He came once to America on business,
long after she was married and had children, and of
course he called. She agreed to meet him between flights,
partly out of curiosity, partly vindication. He looked old,
his hair gray and balding, but the grin was familiar, the
suit still natty tweed. They talked, remembered, he with
crystal clarity, she impressionistically. "So much of what
you told me turned out to be true," he said. "I am alone,
just as you predicted. I'll never forget you saying that to
me in a pub one night. 'You'll grow old alone, unloved.
You'll regret your choices one day.'" "Did I say that?"
"That, and a lot more. You taught me so much. Most of
all, the love of a woman for a man. I've never forgotten,
and I never found it like that anywhere else. Still, I have
no regrets. We had a special time together, didn't we?"
She nodded, rising to leave. "And now you're happily
married with children. Just as it should be." "Yes," she
said. "Just as it should be."

Leaving the lounge, she felt his eyes on her back until
she could no longer have been in his view. Perhaps that
was why she held her head high and light, which was also
how she felt. Cleansed. Intact. Well-balanced and firm of
foot. It had been necessary to come. Acknowledgment.
Closure. And so it was ended, and life went on,
unchanged, and ever changing.

KATHRYN
✦ ✧ ✦
The Red Line

She gets on the train at Grosvenor and realizes immediately that she and the woman with the child are the only women in the car. It is the kind of thing she notices. On long journeys it helps to pass the time. With her categorical mind and demographer's training, she likes to imagine the lives of the characters who people her environment. Some of her friends think she should have been a writer.

Sometimes she thinks so too. Like now, when she scans the train and sees the elements of a short story. "A Train of Men" she would call it, if she wrote. There is the Truman Capote look-alike, intense and secretive in his trenchcoat and hat, his nails bitten to the quick. There is the Brinks armored guard who has just emptied the cash machines and now, in the company of his fellow guards, reads silently from a pocket Bible. On the other side of the glass divide, a man stands reading his paper, catching his reflection in the glass and making her wonder whether he is smiling to himself or grimacing in pain. Across from her an old man reads a newspaper. His red speckled face is kind and intelligent. Not like the student with the beat-up sweater and the earring in his left ear. He looks surly, almost threatening.

Maybe, if she wrote, she would write a story about the woman and child sitting across from her. She watches them intensely. The woman, she sees, is dressed in well-worn clothes neatly put together. Her cotton pullover sweater is clean and her jeans have a seam firmly pressed into them. Her hands, with their large knuckles and thick fingers, are those of a woman accustomed to hard work. She wears no jewelry, not even a wedding band. Her hair is dull brown, long and poorly layered. Her smile reveals that she needs dental work. But still she possesses a kind of attractiveness, as if, given a chance, she might be pretty. Perhaps it is the animated way in which she speaks to the child that lends beauty to her face.

"Did you really?" she asks wide-eyed as the little boy whispers something in her ear. "Well, what did you think then?"

The child eagerly takes up her invitation and launches into further detail, squirming in his seat, tucking his foot under himself, then taking it out again. He is a boy of about five, she guesses, wide-eyed and bright, with a dark blond bowled haircut. He makes her think of a Mary Cassatt painting, a rosy-cheeked child looking adoringly at his mother, who seems to have infinite patience.

The woman engages so fully with her child that it is difficult not to watch them. She tries to stop but finds herself mesmerized. This woman is a good mother. She enjoys her child, finds his enthusiasm something to be respected. She is glad to have him there.

Amid the oblivion of the men in the train, the two women smile at each other the way women do when there is a happy child.

Her mind wanders back to Mary Cassatt and then suddenly to flashes of Degas and Gainsborough, and then to Michelangelo's Pietà. She tries again to look away from the woman, embarrassed by the intensity of her own voyeurism, but cannot release herself from their magnetism.

"He's a lovely child," she says.

"Thank you," the mother answers, smiling proudly. "Do you have children?"

"No."

I did. I had one. A girl called Caitlin. She would have been ten but she died of leukemia. That was three years ago. Sometimes I think I can't go on, but of course I do.

But I never stop thinking of her. Never. Oh, I do for a few minutes here and there. But I can never manage it for long. Like this train ride. I thought I might have twenty-one minutes — that's how long it takes from Grosvenor to DuPont Circle — that I wouldn't think of her at all. I would just stare at other people and imagine what their lives were like. But then here you were with that lovely child and I couldn't not think of Caitlin. That's what happens all the time. When I walk down the street, or go shopping, or go into someone's office and they have a picture of their children on the desk. There's always something so that I can't not think of her. It's cruel in a way. But then one has to learn to live with it, doesn't one?"

"No, I'm afraid I don't."

"Well, they're a lot of work, but they're worth it. Isn't that right, Tim?" She squeezes his hand and he grins.

The doors open at Van Ness and the surly student gets off. The guard keeps reading his Bible, and the man whose reflection puzzles her straightens his tie and grimaces. Truman Capote bites his nails. They all had mothers who loved them once when they were pink-cheeked little boys, she thinks. I wonder what became of their mothers. I wonder what little Tim will be like when he grows up, and if he will always love his mother as he does now. I wonder what Caitlin would have been like when she grew up.

"It's for the best that it's been this quick," she remembers the doctor saying as her child lay dying.

"No!" she had snarled at him like an animal emitting sounds from its viscera. Who the hell did he think he was, anyway? She had had flashes of him then, cold and sterile to his wife and children. Not like the nurse who had hugged her and wept, understanding a life of grief and giving, a mother's life.

At Woodley Park, the woman and child rise to get off.

"Have a nice day," the mother says.

"Goodbye."

There aren't really nice days anymore, she thinks. Only days I get through better than others. She sighs.

She rises to be ready for her exit. The Brinks guard puts away his Bible and moves toward the doors with his escort. Truman Capote burrows into his seat as if he will do nothing more with his life than ride the red line for eternity. The ruddy-cheeked man tips his hat, and the grimacer looks at his feet and coughs.

She wonders if Tim and his mother ride the train often. It would be nice, she muses, to see them again one day, to know whatever became of him, instead of just imagining how he would grow.

She suddenly feels exhausted. Tomorrow, she thinks, I'll drive to work. The train lurches to a stop and as the doors open, she follows the Brinks guard, still clutching his Bible, into the bowels of the station. A gaggle of schoolchildren form a gauntlet, and like a ship in a squall, she lowers her head, sets her shoulders, and forges ahead.

MARSHA

◆ ◇ ◆

The Affair

I wish I could say I went to the woods because I'm mad about nature and big on the environment and forest sunsets give me a shiver every time I see one. But I didn't. I went to the woods because I'd met Jake Rivers and I was hot for his buns, which is what really gave me a shiver every time I saw them, hugged though they were by faded blue denim.

Jake is a forest ranger, and while not exactly endowed in either strength or physical stature with the mythical proportions of a Paul Bunyan, he is, nevertheless, one helluva good-looking dude in a woodsy, outdoor kind of way. He's at least six foot two, muscular and lean at the same time, with robin's egg blue eyes that you could die for. His arms are tanned and covered with just the right amount of auburn hair, matching the little tuft that peeks out of his L.L. Bean chamois shirt below his Adam's apple. His tawny face has crevices in the right places — mainly around his mouth when he smiles and next to those watery blue eyes — and his strawberry blond hair falls across his forehead like Robert Redford's does. In short, he is something else to look at.

I met Jake in the village hardware store last summer. I was rummaging through an assortment of picture hooks when he accidentally backed into me with those legendary buns of his.

"Excuse me," he said, a red flush rising up to meet his oceanic eyes. I looked at him and was speechless. It had been a long time since I'd seen such an extraordinary human being. I felt like a schoolgirl. My stomach actually did one of those little flips that it does when you first become aware of your own sexuality. I managed to smile weakly and mutter something like, "No problem." I thought that was the end of it, like coming out of a dream where you want to linger, but a few days later, at a brunch at the O'Neills', he appeared again. This time he smiled at me with a recognition that bordered on the familiar.

"Hey there! How ya' doin'?" he said.

"Fine. Just fine."

"You two know each other?" my husband asked.

"Yes," Jake said.

"No," I said at the same time. "Well, not really. We happened to bump into each other at Poliner's Hardware the other day."

"Literally," Jake offered, laughing.

Then there were proper introductions all the way around and everyone who was unknown to the group said what they did. That's how I came to know that Jake had recently been transferred by the Forest Service. Kitty Slifer was absolutely intrigued with what it meant to be a forest ranger and asked a lot of questions which Jake answered cheerfully and with great authority. It seemed to me that he was enjoying the attention.

"Why don't you come up to the post one day?" he asked Kitty, but oddly enough, he was looking at me. "All of you. I'll be happy to show you around, give you the VIP Nature Tour!"

"Gee," Kitty said with her usual enthusiasm, "that would be terrific. Why don't we take him up on it?"

The husbands agreed that it would be an interesting outing. Then Jim Slifer got up to freshen his screwdriver and the others followed suit. That seemed to end the matter. Until the following Saturday, when Kitty phoned.

"Let's take him up on it," she said, after the usual amenities.

"What?"

"You know. The forest ranger. Let's go on up there. It'll be something different to do, anyway."

I didn't kid myself about why I said yes. I wanted to lay eyes on him again. Pure and simple.

When we got there, he was sitting on his front porch in cutoffs and a T-shirt that said "Shift Happens." A Bud Lite and a Robertson Davies novel formed a still-life on the table.

"San Francisco," he grinned, by way of explaining his T-shirt. "Welcome!"

"Hi," I said feebly, transfixed by his naked arms and legs and the contour of his chest behind the flimsy T.

"I hope you don't mind," Kitty bubbled. "We were out for a drive and thought we'd take you up on your offer of a visit. We can't stay long."

"I don't mind at all," Jake said. "Nice to have company. Would you like me to show you around, or can I offer you a cold drink?"

"Are they mutually exclusive offers?" I asked, regaining some of the cosmopolitan composure for which I am known in certain circles.

"Not at all," he answered, grinning straight at me. "Back in a flash."

Then he disappeared into the bungalow, a restoration log cabin that looked slightly like a house built for Santa's elves. I was dead curious about what the place looked like inside, whether or not it had a woman's touch. He emerged with two beers in his hand and answered my question.

"I'd invite you in but the place is a mess. What my mother used to call 'bachelor breakdown' in my college days. One of these weeks, I'll get it cleaned up."

Jake handed us each a beer and pointed to the left, setting out ahead of us toward a trail that led into the woods. Almost an hour later we emerged from the same place, having made a circular tour of the nature path frequented by Boy Scouts and school science classes.

"Well, I hope that wasn't too much for a first visit," Jake said. He had been lecturing Nature 101 for forty-five minutes non-stop, clearly in love with his subject. "I tend to go on a bit."

Kitty and I assured him that we had loved every minute of it. It was the truth. I *had* loved every single minute of listening to his resonant voice modulate according to the size of the specimen he was describing. I had loved watching him move with such confidence among the flora. I had especially loved it when he crouched on his haunches to point to a minuscule wildflower or an insect, his arm resting on his knee, hand fisted except for the pointer finger.

"I hope you'll come back again," he said as we got into the car. "In any case, I'm sure I'll see you around town." I thought he looked at me then in a rather penetrating way, but I could have been wrong. I had a way of turning absolutely adolescent in his company. But I did not imagine that his hand brushed my shoulder as he popped the lock on my door down. And I most certainly did not imagine the hairs on my neck standing at attention.

Several weeks passed then before we saw each other again. I got the kids settled into their summer programs. Marty went on an extended business trip. I spent the time while he was gone in annual organizing mode, and got my notes together for the educational article I had to produce by September. There wasn't a lot of time left over for romantic fantasy, but I won't say I didn't daydream some about the man up the mountain.

Finally guilt, or some kind of funny feeling, got the better of me and I called my best friend, Margie.

"I need to talk."

"Great. Life's been really dull. I'll be right over."

She laughed when I told her about The Jake Thing. Margie is married to the most prominent lawyer in town — no one would ever suspect that she carried on with an

African student on the side. She listened to my non-story, and then delighted in fueling my fantasies. "Look, honey," she said, "what harm is there in a little flirtation? Enjoy yourself!"

Not a week later, Jake showed up in my aisle at the grocery store.

"Hey!" he said, which seemed to be his usual greeting.

"Well, hello there." I smiled, genuinely glad to see him (which, of course, came as no surprise).

"You know, I've been meaning to get in touch. There's the most incredible family of black bears up on the mountain. I made a sort of dugout where I can watch them undetected. I thought you might like to take a look. I mean, you seemed pretty interested in all that nature stuff when you were up." He had an extraordinary way of making everything seem so interesting that you would be a fool to miss it.

"That sounds fascinating. Maybe I should bring my kids up," I said, testing the waters.

"Well, that would be okay, I guess. But too many people at one time could be a bit dangerous."

Right. "Oh, I see."

"Whatever suits you best. Hope to see you!" He waved and pushed his cart down the aisle.

When I got home I put the ice cream away and called Margie.

"Help!" I said. "I think I'm getting into something here that I may live to regret."

Her advice was predictable. "Just go and see what happens. At least, you'll get it out of your system. Why not spend a couple of days at our cabin?"

By the time Marty got back, I had the whole thing worked out in my mind. I had decided that Margie was right. I needed to get it out of my system, whatever "it" was. And the only way I was going to do that successfully was to plunge into whatever had taken hold of me that day in the hardware store, let it play itself out, and exorcise it.

I am an English teacher and occasionally I write short articles for academic journals, so it was easy enough for me to say I was going to the mountain for a few days to "work on a piece" at Margie's weekend cabin. I even had myself convinced that that was my mission. After all, what else could a nearly middle-aged, slightly overweight, beginning to gray mother of three expect, really? Marty didn't bat an eye. He was used to me seeking seclusion when I had work to do.

"That'll be good for you," he said when I shared my plan with him. "The kids and I will hold down the fort, don't you worry." What a sweet man he is, I thought as I packed the car the following Saturday. What the hell am I doing here?

The drive up the mountain was glorious. I felt freer than I had for years, as if suddenly I had been cast upon the earth for an odyssey with my name on it. I had a vision of myself being ten pounds lighter, with no gray hairs, and not a wrinkle on my face. The very thought of it made me laugh out loud.

When I got to Margie's cabin, I opened the door and all the windows and in no time at all, the place was full of the freshness of a pine forest. Also in no time at all, I had a visitor. I was unpacking when he appeared, grinning, at the screen door.

"What'd you do? Run away from home?"

"Not exactly. Just took a leave of absence. Want a beer?"

"Sure."

I took two Buds out of the cooler and handed him one, letting the screen door slam behind me. "I hope the bears are still around."

"That why you came?"

"Actually, I came up to get some work done. Anyway, what are you doing here?"

"I saw your car come up the road. Just wanted to make sure everything was all right."

"Oh. I see. It's reassuring to have good neighbors."

"Listen, I promise not to bug you. What are you working on?" He leaned his chair back against the porch rail-
ing and spread his legs to keep his balance. The sun
caught the golden hairs on his legs. It took everything
I've got to keep my eyes above his waist. I told him about
the article I was writing, an academic piece about
Victorian women writers and how what they wrote was
different from how they lived. He seemed genuinely
interested and surprisingly well read. He even asked
some questions about Austen and the Brontes; I was
impressed. But I wanted to stay visceral.

"So what about the bears?"

"Oh, they're fine. Want to go out and see them this
evening? That's the best time to catch them, actually."

"Sure. That would be great."

"Listen, I have an idea," he said, putting his chair back
on all fours and looking me square in the eye. "I've got
some leftover chili and a half-decent bottle of Chianti.
Why not go on a bear safari, say about seven, and then
have dinner? You can start working tomorrow."

"Sounds good to me," I grinned. In fact, it sounded
wonderful.

I finished putting away the groceries, set up my
portable PC, and unpacked my clothes. I made the bed
and cut some flowers from in front of the cabin which I
plunked in a glass on the table. Then I drew the water for
a bath, throwing in some of Margie's bath beads. I wonder how often she brings her African up here, I mused,
lying in the luxury of the tub. What they get up to; what
they actually DO? My fantasies got pretty wild. And then
it wasn't Margie and her African I was daydreaming
about. It was me, and that stud of a forest ranger.

I got out of the tub and with a towel wrapped around
me, went to peruse my limited wardrobe. I had one skirt
with me, a floral print. Slightly too Laura Ashley, but I
dressed it down with a pastel pink cotton sweater, sandals,
and large gold hoop earrings. I put on a good whop of
deodorant since I was already sweating the way I do when

I'm nervous, a touch of make-up, and one whiff of First cologne. I brushed my hair and roughed it up with my fingers. Then I decided the skirt would never do for bear-watching and switched to jeans.

I drove to Jake's cabin so that I wouldn't have to walk back alone in the dark. He was on the porch, leaning against a post with one arm raised, the other in his hip pocket. He was wearing newly washed faded denims and a cotton shirt with tiny blue and white squares on it. It had epaulets and the sleeves were rolled up to just below the elbow. His feet were bare. He was gorgeous.

"Howdy, Neighbor," he grinned at me.

I smiled back. "Hi." I always seemed to be reduced to monosyllables whenever I tried talking to Jake. He didn't seem to mind.

"How 'bout a drink before we go bear hunting?"

My scotch and water and his beer came out on a tray this time. There was even a dish of olives and some crackers in a bowl. He was obviously in entertaining mode. We sipped our drinks and made small talk. Then he said decisively, "Let's go before it's too dark."

We made for the path where Kitty and I had had our nature tour, but just before it headed into the woods, Jake put his hand on my back to steer me to the right. He kept it there so that he could guide me to his dugout. I wished we'd never get there.

It was a winding path thick with growth. We ducked and pushed branches out of our way as if they were huge garden gates opening onto Eden. Then, suddenly, there was a clearing, and the trench. It was small. I knelt into it first, then Jake squinched in. His chest pressed against my back, warm and pulsing. It was like the way Marty and I sleep, back to front. I felt horrendously aroused and guilty at the same time.

"Are you okay?" Jake asked.

"Yes, fine," I said, breathless.

We stayed in that position for fifteen or twenty minutes. My legs were cramped but I didn't want to get up, ever. The bears never showed. "This is a ruse," I said, beginning to giggle. "There aren't any bears!"

"No, no! I swear! Maybe they'll be back tomorrow," Jake laughed. He stood up and pulled me to my feet. For a second it was like a hug. I wanted to kiss him.

"Well, there better be some chili, that's all I can say," I joked, pushing my hair back and trying to regain my composure. Jake put his hand on my neck and gave it a shake, the way you would a child who was a little out of line.

We walked back to his cabin, quiet against the silence of the woods but for the bird sounds. The evening sky was periwinkle blue and pink. For a moment, I felt enormously sad. I often feel like that when the sun is setting. This time, though, it was different, deeper.

He saw it. "Penny for your thoughts."

"No way. They're worth a lot more. Believe me, you can't afford it." Both of us knew where that could take us. Mercifully, we were at the cabin by then.

We set the picnic table on the porch and wolfed our chili with garlic bread and salad. "I'm starved!" Jake said, grinning, during a pause for seconds. I nodded concurrence, my mouth swilling Chianti. When we were satiated, we slowed down to a leisurely pace of bread nibbling. Jake opened a second bottle of wine. It was going to be a long evening.

We sat there for hours, talking. God, did we talk! Everything from family history to politics to films to whatever. In all the hours Jake and I ended up spending together last summer and into the year, we never ran out of things to talk about. In the beginning, he was Hemingwayesque; minimal. Like, "I was married once. For seven years. Now I'm not. It doesn't matter about what happened in between." Later he talked more and I learned how hurt he was when his wife left him for another man. I learned a lot about him over time. But that night on his porch, it wasn't such personal talk. Just friendly talk. And flirtation, like Margie said. Two people getting to know each other, liking each other, wanting each other.

It must have been four in the morning when I first began making mild sounds about having to leave. At six, when the sun was truly up, I left. He wanted to see me back but I knew neither one of us would get any work done, and I had the car, so I said no. "Catch you later," I said, cavalierly, and waved as I drove off.

Back in my own cabin, I flopped onto the bed and was asleep in no time. It was a short nap. I won't say it was the first time I've ever woken up to a dream-induced orgasm all by myself, but it sure was the best. I tried desperately to re-enter the dream. We were somewhere, Jake and me, in a big tent with the flaps open. We were clothed, but in the throes of extraordinary foreplay. Then I realized (in the dream) that there were black bears cavorting play-fully in and out of the tent but I didn't care. They were sort of pets and we weren't afraid of them. It was like Nirvana. I could smell the air, see the sky, hear the birds, feel his hands between my legs. That's when I was forced into semi-consciousness and when I went incredibly over the edge. I lay there panting afterward, trying to recap-ture the pleasure of the dream. I imagined what it would really be like to lie naked with him. I wanted to feel his body against mine. I wanted to have him stroke me every-where until I couldn't stand it anymore. I wanted to wrap my legs around his torso as he came into me. I wanted to make love to this man, passionately, and without the pre-dictability of a familiar partner.

For a very long time I lay with those thoughts, until I drifted once again into sleep. When I opened my eyes again, it was nearly noon. Christ, I thought, this will not do. I got up, brewed a pot of strong coffee, and drank a mug full of it while I ran a bath and made the bed. Then, bathed and dressed in fresh shorts and T-shirt, I went to the PC and started rummaging through my notes. By an act of extraordinary will, I stayed there, actually working, until just after five, when Jake appeared at the door, breathless and excited. "They're back!" he wheezed. "The bears!"

So off we raced to the dugout, taking up our sandwich position, and sure enough, there they were, three furry balls cavorting like the black bears of my dream and us not being afraid, just enjoying it, without the foreplay part.

Dinner was on me that night. We grilled hamburgers and ate on my porch and talked again into the night and wanted each other but said goodbye with nothing more than a kiss and a long embrace. It went on like that the whole time I was at the cabin, me working, feeling my want of him build until we were finally together in the evening in friendship and restraint. On the last night, we talked about it. I told him I just couldn't "do it," mostly because I didn't want to chance losing what was between us, our special bond, and because Marty didn't deserve it either. He understood. I think he was afraid, too, that sex might contaminate the friendship that felt so important to both of us. And weird as it sounds, I think it was the wanting of each other that both of us were enjoying so much.

I went back up the mountain as often as I could that summer, always with the anticipation of a schoolgirl. And I was never disappointed. Being with Jake was special every time. After a while, the sexual attraction began to subside, although it never faded altogether. Every time he kissed me goodbye I vaguely regretted not having made love with him.

Once school started, I couldn't make it very often. He came into town sometimes and we would meet for lunch. It was during one of those lunches, in February or March, that he told me he was leaving. And about Jenny. "She's so much younger than me, I must be nuts," he said, with his Robert Redford grin. He was obviously smitten. In June they left for Brazil, and some sort of scientific expedition into the rain forest. He promised to stay in touch. I did too.

I still think about him a lot. Every time I go into Poliner's Hardware and sometimes at the grocery store. I missed him at the O'Neills' annual brunch. Sometimes I do a double-take when I see a guy in a pair of faded denims from behind. This summer has a kind of empty feeling to it. I told Margie about it. She understood; her African graduated and left too. The only part she couldn't quite get was how you could have an affair without ever taking your clothes off. I have the feeling, although I never tell her, that in some kind of important way, mine was a lot better than hers.

MARTA
✦ ✧ ✦
A Hole in the Hill

Thirty-six days. Eternity. That's how long we've been in Henri's flat, waiting to be rescued.

Three nights ago a runner came and said we must all go to the shelter because heavy mortar fire was expected. We debated and argued about it. Henri was adamant. "I'm not leaving!" he shouted at George, who thought we should all go down. I knew he wouldn't budge. I decided to stay in the flat with him. George took Nadia and Tania. Just before they left, we embraced. Nadia's eyes were full of despair. I kissed her cheek, and the baby's. "It will be all right," I whispered in her ear. "Don't be afraid."

When they'd gone, Henri and I exchanged worried glances, but neither of us spoke. I felt like the captain putting everyone else in the lifeboats and then waiting for the ship to go down. But there was also a certain calm, a peacefulness, as if once the guests had gone we could kick off our shoes. Henri drew the heavy drapes and we lit one of the last two candles we could find. Then we sat on the floor on big cushions, shoulder to shoulder, knees drawn up, in front of the sofa. He lit two cigarettes and passed me one.

"What do you make of it, Marta?" he asked. "What do you really think is going to happen?"

"I think either we are going to live, or we are going to die. In either case, it will be a terrible winter."

"It's a bitch," he said.

"Yes. A real bitch."

Henri looked at me with that smile, at once cynical and pathetic. "You know," he said, "I believe that it won't be long before the whole world is living once again in clans, bartering beads for bread. God knows, raping and pillaging is back." He paused. "How is it that civilization never really progresses?"

With that, a huge explosion rocked the building's foundation. Bits of plaster fell from the ceiling and a picture dropped to the floor, its glass smashing.

"My God, that was close!" I sputtered, putting my hand on Henri's knee to help boost me up.

"Where the hell are you going?" Henri asked.

"I'll be right back. Don't go away."

A minute later I returned with a bottle of 1986 Chateauneuf de Pape. "I've been waiting for just the right occasion," I said, waving the bottle at him.

"Marta, you are a woman of valor and a true friend!" Henri slapped my knee as I settled down on the floor again.

The next shell was further away, lobbed from the mountains that surround the city into a distant neighborhood.

"I used to play in those mountains when I was a girl," I told Henri. "We used to go on weekends to a small 'dacha' that my father had built, my sisters, my cousins, and I. We played war games in the caves that dot the hills. We called them 'the holes in the hills.' Everything seems a game when you are young."

"Why did you come back, Marta? I mean, after you went to study abroad?"

"I fell in love with a great socialist. He and I, and I suppose many others like us, had wonderful plans for rebuilding this country. He was to follow me after completing his graduate studies. But on the way, he discovered capitalism and got diverted and in the end, he never made it."

"It must have been a great disappointment for you."

"Yes. But this is also my home. And I'm not complaining. I had some very good love affairs in my day."

"And children, a family?" Henri asked.

"My students became my children, my family."

Then another blast, quite close, silenced us. We sipped our wine, which had gone slightly sour with age.

I lit another cigarette.

We still can't believe what is happening. It seems like yesterday we were a city like any other, people working, laughing, arguing, making love, complaining that the bus is late or the soup is cold. Today we are under siege for reasons we can't understand. For years, we lived together peacefully. Now, all of a sudden, our friends, our neighbors, our co-workers are the enemy. We don't know what is to become of us. We are lost. Life is suddenly barbaric, medieval.

It's almost unbearable at times. The men stalk like caged animals, drawing on their cigarettes as if they were opium. Nadia and I talk quietly, about the baby, about life before we descended into hell. Before the occupation, we were on polite terms, she and I, but without much in common. But since our confinement, she has been like a best friend, despite the difference in our ages. Also like a daughter. When I could see that she was frightened, about to weep, I would put my arm around her as though she were a child. Once, she let her head rest on my shoulder and I could feel her weariness and pain. It was all I could do not to cry myself. But I am careful not to let my own anxiety and fear overwhelm me. The others look to me, and Henri, for hope. But sometimes, I want to scream, tear at my hair. I feel trapped, on the verge of hysteria. Other times, I am calm, amazingly stoic, resigned to fate. What does it matter in the end, really, I ask myself. We will all die one day, in one way or another. Are we to be pitied any more than the starving masses, or the millions of victims who preceded us in history, or a poor chap dying of cancer?

I flicked the ashes from my cigarette into a saucer overflowing with butts. Henri looked at me and let out a long sigh, as if to say, "why bother cleaning it up?"

The world has forgotten us, or tries to ignore us. It's extraordinary. We hear sometimes on the wireless that there are discussions and debates, but what good is that when you are about to be annihilated? Don't they understand what is happening here? Of course, we have nothing to offer, no political or economic collateral, only human beings dying for no reason other than greed and power.

Sometimes in the midst of our boredom and fear, there is rage. A while back, Henri nearly exploded. He was peeking through the curtain into the darkness when a shell whizzed in the distance and hit a building in a burst of light. Suddenly, he whirled around. "Christ!" he shouted, his arm shooting up to his shaft of unruly hair. "This isn't goddamn 1812 or 1942! What the hell is going on here?" Then he calmed down and looked around at us, his startled audience, and grinned that lopsided smile of his that makes everything he says seem ironic. "'War is hell,'" he said, smirking sadly.

Henri is provocative but gentle. A combination of decent humanity, a keen intellect, and youthful impatience. He is barely 30 years old, an artist who illustrates magazines and textbooks for a living. He is not very good looking. Too lean and shaggy and slightly stooped, as if his 6'2" frame were too big for the world. His clothes are always rumpled and his cheeks are slightly sunken. But there is something very attractive, sensual, about him. If I were younger, I could fall in love with him.

It was natural that we should congregate in Henri's flat when the trouble started. It's where we always gravitated for a celebration or when there was bad news. Either his place or mine, but he's ground floor and I'm third. I suppose that's because we are the take-charge ones in our small cooperative apartment block, he because he is forceful and outraged by injustice, me because I am something of a matriarch, and considered a no-nonsense lady — The Professor.

The first few nights, we were all stunned, terrified by the shelling. With every crackling explosion we offered a unified gasp of horror, like a religious chant. Fortunately the baby, Tania, was young enough to sleep through most of it. She only cried for the usual things, to be fed or held or made dry. It would be dreadful to have toddlers or other children here to echo the whining of the bombs. But as the weeks have gone on, we hardly cringe. It's amazing what the human mind and body can endure, adjust to. After a while, we tried to go back to our own flats, but then we returned to Henri's. It's easier to bear if you are with others. Everyone has to put up a good front, and there is at least the political discussion to liven things up. We have also pooled our supplies, but still they are running out. We've taken to reusing tea bags, and poor Nadia was reduced two weeks ago to using rags for sanitary napkins.

Not long ago, we had a scare. Armund went on a bread run and didn't come back. Later, we heard that a group of people waiting for bread had been fired on. We thought he was dead. But then we got word from one of the street runners — the boys who run messages from one building to another — that he had made it to safety in a colleague's flat.

We are a compatible group, bonded by our liberal attitudes and our striving for middle-class lives. We have all lived in this building long enough to feel like family. There are only five flats, so we know each other quite well. With Armund elsewhere, it was only Henri, Nadia, George and the baby, and myself these last nights. Suzanna and Josef went to the country before the trouble started and are stranded there, and the small flat has been vacant since Mrs. Poznik died. A lucky thing for whoever might have taken it, thinking how well situated we are, in the city and on the main line to the airport.

Henri and I spent the night, sitting on the floor like that, smoking, thinking, talking a little, until the second candle had burned down, the wine was long finished, and daylight began to put an end to the horrendous sounds of shelling. I was just getting up to see about some tea when the runner arrived. The look on his face was horrible. Contorted, almost grotesque.

"What is it?" Henri demanded.

"It's . . . it's . . . My God, it's too awful! I can hardly say it!"

"Speak, man!" Henri shouted.

"It's Nadia. Tania."

"Oh, my God!" I grabbed onto Henri's arm.

"A shell. It hit the bunker. Many people were hurt. Some killed. Nadia and Tania. They're both dead!"

"Oh God! Oh God, no!" Henri crossed himself.

I stood in disbelief. Numb. Unable to feel. "George?"

"He's like a crazy man. Running around the street, clutching the baby, when I left." Then he collapsed into tears, this child of fifteen, who had seen it all.

Later, Henri brought George back to the flat. A doctor we know came to give him some sleeping tablets and told us to watch him carefully. When he awoke, he was quite calm and lucid. I gave him some tea and a biscuit and put my arms around him. We wept, the three of us together, in a huddle of misery.

"I will carry Tania's coffin myself at the funeral," George said. "I would like you, dear Henri and Marta, to help carry Nadia. Of course, I will quite understand if you would rather not come out for the funeral." His voice was frighteningly guttural, as if it came from someone else.

"We will be there," Henri said simply.

The funeral is today. We are waiting now to leave. Armund will go with us, and then we will come back to the flat, to wait again, for what, we do not know.

Yesterday, Gila, Henri's young friend who aspires to be a poet, came to see us. She said she had managed to get a letter out, to an Israeli writer who is in charge of a poetry conference that will soon take place in Jerusalem. "Tell the world what is happening here," she wrote. "Write about us so that we are not forgotten. Tell them about Nadia and Tania and the others. Pray for us."

We don't expect we shall ever hear back. But it was a gesture toward humanity, and for a moment, it gave us all a glimmer of hope.

CARA
✦ ✧ ✦
Leaning Into the Light

A long time ago, when I was young and time was something we all took for granted, a friend of mine robbed me of summers. Every June she declared that once July 4th arrived, it seemed like the summer was over. That pronouncement never failed to overcome me like the heat of a Charleston afternoon in August. I would drag myself through the long, seemingly last days of summer, limp with perspiration, and well before Labor Day loomed, mourn the end of the season of my freedom. And no matter how many more summers passed, full of languid, golden days beyond our independence celebrations, with their lemon chiffon picnics and raucous parades to prove her wrong, I never truly recovered my sense of lost time. It has followed me all the days of my life — until now — so that once Labor Day came it seemed to be Christmas, and at Christmas I began to think of Easter, and Easter reminded me that soon it would be July 4th, and the end of summer.

I think of those days now, as I languish in my reprieve, a 52-year-old woman who has been told her days are well and truly numbered. Or at least her years. Or months. Who knows really? Perhaps I will prove them wrong. In a strange sort of way, I almost don't care, because I have come to accept it now, and to love my living so much that time is meaningless, a useless man-made construct, it seems to me, with its nullifying linearity, its confines, its one-directional, one-dimensional intensity, its stifling demands. I no longer hate time. I am oblivious to it. And I know now that one should never be its slave.

Of course, it took my illness, and my age, I suppose, to know this. Before they cut off my breast and then told me that my bones were "involved," I would never have thought these things, never have known what I know now. I would not have realized, for example, how long the smell of incense lasts, nor would I have appreciated the way a rose feels like velvet when you brush it against your cheek. I wouldn't have sat for hours watching a ballet of tree boughs, or listened in the early morning for the joyous cacophony of bird sounds. I wouldn't have realized how much I love the taste of salt water from the sea on my lips. And I wouldn't have heard the spirits when they soul-talk me. Nor would I have known Marcus.

Marcus is one of my spirit voices. He came to me the first day I was on this island, which I would not have come to if it hadn't been for the stalking monster waiting to claim me. I would have said I couldn't afford the time to come and sit idly day after day on a lovely Greek island in the middle of the diamond-studded Aegean Sea. I would have thought myself too busy with the trivia of my executive, city life to savor — to utterly embrace — the warm moist air of a summer evening in the land of the gods, to sip endless cups of hot, strong coffee in the morning as I watch the boatmen ready themselves for the day, or to nurse a goblet of barely chilled white wine when they come home at night.

That was how I first met Marcus. I was sitting outside the fishermen's cafe one evening some weeks, perhaps a month ago — who knows? — watching them clean and mend their nets when he smiled up at me from his boat. It was a casual, honest smile and I smiled back and continued to watch him and the older men work. He was lovely, tan and muscular in his cutaway shirt and faded jeans. His face was broad and square, his features deep set and dark, his hands quick and sure. I liked the way he moved, his body a continuous flow of choreographed activity.

After a while, when he had finished, he climbed out of the boat and onto the dock in a single pirouette. Then he came straight toward me, grinning, and sat down at my table as if I'd been waiting for him all the while.

"I get so thirsty at the end of the day," he said. A teasing grin played across his face, pushing his rosy, sunburnt cheeks up toward laugh lines that splayed out from his eyes. "I'll join you, yes?"

"Yes," I said.

It was that simple.

In the beginning, I continued meeting him at the fishermen's cafe when his boat came in because of the simple joy of watching him. I loved seeing him move his young, lithe, healthy body against a sky turning pink and lavender, as I loved listening to his deep voice and resonant laughter when he told me village stories and Greek legends over a glass of wine. And yes, I loved the warmth of his body next to mine, the touch of his arm when it inadvertently rubbed against my own, the smell of his sweat, beading on his neck and forming dark V-shaped stains down the back of his shirt. It made me want to taste him with a sensuality I had not felt since long before my surgery and the pain that now invades my body when I am weary, or allow myself to feel self-pity.

But after a few times like that, just being together, suspended in a magic moment of friendship, of mutuality, of sensual connection, something changed, deepened. I felt it as clearly as if I had been physically transformed by some natural force, a great wind which had blown over me so that my contours were no longer the same, changed invisibly, and irrevocably. He felt this thing too, and once he said, suddenly and with great joy, "Cara, I am so alive in these moments with you!"

Before death forced me into life, I would have thought this all outrageous. Nothing more than a pathetic flirtation on my part, a gigolo's jest on his. I would have asked stupid questions of him, and myself, designed to demonstrate that I knew the rigid rules of conduct in what we fight to convince ourselves is a sane world. I would have said, "But this is ridiculous! I'm old enough to be your mother! It's all very flattering, but really . . . I know what you're after."

Instead, I loved him.

The first time I didn't feel well enough to come to the cafe was when I knew Marcus was a soul-spirit. He came to my villa to look for me, tracing the steps we had taken together when he walked me home once. How I loved that walk in the mornings, and in the evenings! Up the cobblestoned hill, past the church with its bent women in black clutching their rosaries as they struggled up and down the steep steps to bargain with Christ, down past the shops with their tempting oranges and bottles of wine and pastries, into the square where restaurants served endless Greek salads and *dolmatis* to camera-laden tourists in straw hats, and finally to the quay where colorful fishing boats like Marcus's bobbed in the water as if to say "Now? Can we go now?"

When he arrived, I was sitting on the veranda on a chaise with a book in my hand but my eyes were closed and I was listening to the sound of the water lapping gently onto the beach so that I did not hear him approach.

"Cara?" he said gently. It sounded like a prayer.

I opened my eyes and felt the pleasure rise in my body from my stomach to my chest to my head.

"Marcus! I'm glad to see you."

"Are you all right? Why you did not come to the cafe?" he asked.

"Marcus. I think we must talk," I said, lowering my legs from the chaise so that he could sit by me.

"I know what you are going to say, Cara," he said, lowering himself gracefully onto the chaise. "I am too young, and you are too old, and you have been thinking it over, and . . ."

"Well, there is that," I said, smiling at him. I took his hand and kissed his palm before pressing it to my cheek. "But there is something else. Something much bigger than all of that, I'm afraid."

"What are you saying?" He looked at me with timeless, infinite eyes.

"In a moment. But first, I want you to know . . ."

"I know. I know, Cara. Do you not think it is the same for me?"

I looked at him, at his lovely, classical, kouros face, and what filled my senses was a mixture of such exquisite joy, love, and pure beauty that despite its pain, I would have frozen that moment into all eternity if I could have. Then, I took his hand and placed it on my empty chest, where once there had been a full, round breast, but where now only a scar resided.

He didn't flinch. He didn't instinctively pull back his hand in horror, or shock, or even because it intruded. Instead, ever so slowly, with his other hand, he gently opened the buttons on my shirt and then, pulling the fabric aside, bent and kissed my absent breast. Only then did he raise his eyes to mine, and whisper, "Cara. My Cara," taking me into his arms and stroking my hair as he rocked me back and forth as if I were a child who had lost her mother.

No one has ever made love to me the way Marcus did that day, and since. No one has ever made my body come so alive that it quivers itself into birth over and over again until the ripples of satisfaction go from my toes straight into the soul of the cosmos. No one has ever made me feel so beautiful, so whole, so pure. And no man I know has ever been able to do with his own body the things that Marcus does, things that bring us to such wholeness, such unity that I feel I shall wake in some spirit place never before trodden upon.

After that first time, we talked long into the night and the next day, the breeze fluttering in through windows flagrantly flung open so that we could drink in the sea air and feel its moisture on our naked skin. When we ate, we sat on the veranda wrapped in white sheets like ancient gods. It was during one of those times that I asked him why he came to sit with me that first evening in the cafe.

"I looked up," he said, "and you were in the light."

"Yes?"

"That is how I try to live my life. Always leaning into the light."

As my darkness approaches, that is also how I want to live my life. Leaning into the light.

In different times, I would worry that having Marcus stay with me would be scandalous. "What will people say!" It is a question I ask him, actually. This is, after all, his village.

"Cara!" he says then, mockingly. "You are older, therefore you should be wiser. What is age? What is time?" Then, if we are in bed, he runs his finger along my scar, drawing imaginary flowers along its stem. "What is beauty?"

When we are playful like that, we think about what is coming. We have talked about it, and we know that I am thinner, more tired, weaker as time goes on. I manage the pain with very little medication. I think it would be worse if I were not so oddly happy, so utterly at peace, even though my heart is breaking.

But the day is coming, and we both know that.

When I first came here, I thought it was only for a short while, to face the demon of death on my own terms. Somehow, I thought, I would make myself ready to die, and then I would go home to do it with grace — completely in control — because that was, after all, what people would expect of me.

But now, I make no decisions. I don't plan. I have no arrangements. I feel no obligation. Every day, I just lean farther into the light. I push the edge of summer. I live.

I doubt that anyone back in the city, or in the Charleston of my childhood, would understand any of this. But Marcus does. I do. And in this moment of our being, and our being together, that is enough for us.

DANIELLE
✦ ✧ ✦
Déjà Vu

Darling! You're miles away! What were you thinking?"
James asks. We are sitting in a cafe on the Champs-
Elysées, having strong, dark coffee as we always do on our
first afternoon in Paris.

"I was just thinking how it's changed. So crowded, so
dilapidated somehow. I can never come to Paris without
remembering the days when I first saw it. God, it was
beautiful! The elegance! I wept the first time I saw the
Eiffel Tower."

"Yes, my love. You tell me that every time we come.
And I remind you that for all your socialist tendencies,
you don't really like it that the masses can now afford to
live like you do. Well, almost."

I decline the bait. We've had this pseudo-argument
enough times by now that it is no longer amusing for
either of us. Besides, in a moment James will excuse himself to attend his first meeting. And I will linger in the
cafe, remembering.

1966. The Grand Tour the way students did it in those
days: *Frommer's Guide to Europe on $5 a Day,* a Eurorail pass,
good walking shoes, and a backpack on your shoulder. I
had elected to visit only three countries during my
month's excursion, beginning in England.

We met on the boat-train from London to Paris. He
was on his way back to Ankara from the London School

of Economics for the summer holiday.

It's a long journey from the austere, well-behaved capital of Great Britain to the melancholy sweetness of Paris. The train winds through lush green English countryside, fresh with the scent of wetness and newly mown fields. The Channel ferry makes its voyage in slow and rolling heaves, like an overweight peasant woman bored with her endless plowing. We sat in deck chairs on that sun-sprayed summer day and dipped into our souls in rhythm with the undulating sea. On the train to Paris, we were silent much of the time, but with the pleasure of pausing, and not the embarrassment of having nothing more to say.

There were three glorious days in Paris. We picnicked in the Tuileries on bread and cheese with strawberries and wine. We marveled together at the Mona Lisa, strolled this very avenue at midnight, sipped cappuccino at sidewalk cafes. On the Left Bank, we ate *cervelles de veau* sauteed in butter, savored the bouquet in a glass of Blanc de Blanc, peered over the shoulders of street artists, and then made love.

"L'addition, Madame?" the waiter asks. How long has he been hovering? I hand him a hundred francs. "Merci," he says, swooping up my demitasse, a signal for me to vacate the table. I decide to walk down the Champs-Elysées to the Tuileries.

The boulevard is crowded with people, an amalgam of weary, smartly dressed Parisians and tourists, the young ones draped around each other in unisex trousers and jackets, some with jaunty hats or cigarettes dripping from their lips. Cars and buses belch smoke as they weave their way to somewhere. An occasional tri-color flag snaps flamboyantly in the breeze. Pigeons strut like impresarios.

I have grown tired of these trips. They are always the same. Capital cities viewed from the back seat of a taxi or limousine, world-class hotels with sterile lobbies of mauve and lime green, elegant dining rooms staffed by mute

waiters, boutique shops where saleswomen in under-
stated Chanel suits serve the clientele, charming conversation between clever wives, appendages who know their
place in their husbands' lives. I suppose in the beginning,
I found it all fascinating. But that was a long time ago,
and now, I don't actually remember. It's just the way it is.

At the foot of the Champs-Elysées, just before the gar-
dens start, I stop to peer in the window of a china shop. It
has a special display of objets d'art. They are all made of
Murano glass.

Our itineraries crossed again in Venice a week after we
left Paris. I wandered aimlessly en route through Florence
and Rome and then once in Venice, went straight to our
meeting place in San Marco Square. I was heartbroken
when he did not appear at the appointed time. Then the
next morning, while I was having brioche and strong coffee on the terrace of my pensione, he came through the
portal like a Turkish icon smiling in slow motion. "I
missed the train!" he exclaimed, pressing me to him,
laughing. "Did you really think I wouldn't come?"

Our time in Venice mirrored that of Paris — long, languid days punctuated by bursts of energy and spirited
exploration, tender moments, unfettered joy. Exploring
the city's medieval magic, we crisscrossed the labyrinth of
canals, dined on terraced piazzas, strolled the alleyways.
One day, we took a *vaporetto* to Lido, and it was there he
bought me the red Murano glass swan.

"Because you are a *kugu*," he said. "A swan."

"If I am a swan," I laughed, "then surely you are an
eagle."

"A *kartal*!" He rolled his dark eyes and grinned.

Two days later, we parted at the train station. "I know
we will be together again," he said as he kissed me goodbye.

The Tuileries are peaceful and quiet, a welcome respite from urban chaos. Dotted by old men with their chins resting on their chests, matrons strolling arm in arm, young mothers watchful of playing children, lovers gliding hand in hand, the walkways crunch under the weight of their visitors. Shade trees bend in the wind like cavalier courtiers. Long-stemmed flowers nod as if having an afternoon doze. I sit on a bench trying to clear my mind. Soon it will be time to dress for dinner.

On the way back to our hotel, I stop at the Cafe Fournier. Suddenly, I feel weary, laden with weight. The waiter smiles as though he too is exhausted. "Oui, Madame," he says to greet me. "Thé, s'il vous plait," I say. I peruse the crowded tables, their animated occupants adding to the importance of what they say by sweeping gestures of their manicured hands. The sound of impeccable French is a pleasant din to my untrained ear.

The waiter brings the tea and I reach for a sugar cube with silver tongs. That is when I see him.

At first, it's only the back of a head and then a partial side view. I start, think myself crazy. I have been daydreaming too long, I think. But then, he turns, and I see his full face. It is rounder now, fleshed out by time and the good life, but they are the same dark and dancing eyes, and isn't the smile the dimpled one I knew? I feel certain. His hair is thinning, receding back from above each eyebrow, but still curly. His cheeks above the beard line are still the color of blush and excitement. I watch. He is seated with two other men, portly business types in silk suits. One of them writes on a notepad and nods in punctuation. Although I cannot hear them clearly, they are speaking a language other than French.

An idea crosses my mind. I quickly dismiss it. Then the waiter asks me if there will be anything else. I pause. "Non, merci." Then, "Mais, oui," I hear myself say, and, trembling, I ask him to wait a moment. I open my purse and take out a writing pad and pen. On a slip of paper I write, "After these many years, the *kugu* sends greetings to the *kartal.*" I ask the waiter to hand it to the gentleman, pointing. He moves toward their table. My heart pounds. I cannot believe I have done such a thing. But I am so certain, and surely, one cannot let pass a moment like this.

He takes the note, listens to something the waiter whispers in his ear, and then puzzled, glances at me. There is no recognition. He reads what I have written. Nothing. He smiles weakly in my direction. The waiter disappears discreetly. I turn away.

I leave the money for my tea on the table and weave my way to the exit, head down. Outside, the air soothes me like a compress on my forehead. By the time I reach the George V, I am breathless. Perspiration runs down my back and between my breasts. The hotel doorman tips his hat, opens the door. I make for the elevator.

In the room, the message light flashes on the telephone. It is from James. "Dinner at eight. Formal."

I go to the closet, take out the taffeta and velvet Givenchy, draw a bath. When James arrives, I am putting on my earrings.

"Good day?" he asks.

I nod.

He changes into his tux. In the elevator, we are silent. Outside, the limousine is waiting.

THEO
✦ ✧ ✦
Undercurrents

On a morning not long after her eighteenth anniversary, Theo Maizel wakes knowing that the dark side of marriage has finally overtaken her. Marriages are like people, she thinks, rubbing the sleep out of her eyes. They have their black sinister side, even though others may never see their underbelly, may not know about its shadow. But that shadow lurks there all the same, and one day, under just the right circumstances, its darkness intrudes upon the psyche so that things are never the same again.

She raises herself against the disheveled pillows of the king-size bed she shares with Noah and watches the newly hatched leaves on the trees outside their bedroom window sway lazily in the early spring breeze. She tries to cling to the anesthesia of deep sleep on her day off, but it is after nine. Noah is long gone to catch the 7:36 into the city and her three self-sufficient teenage children have gotten themselves off to school as they always do. Now, as last evening's events flash into memory, her mind wanders, replaying random scenes from her marriage. Images parade before her relentlessly, and the disturbing thing is that all the recollections flooding her psyche are negative portraits, as if her brain were a disc on which all the positive files have suddenly been deleted. She remembers the time Noah scolded her, just after they were married, for keeping him waiting at a restaurant, even though he knew she was shopping with his sister and must have been detained. He spoke to her then as if she were a child. "Don't do that again!" he said, but as usual when he was displeased with her, she remained silent. Once, when she complained that he was working later and later so that they had no time together, he snapped, "Don't push me!" wagging his forefinger and lecturing on the quality of their future if he worked hard at this stage of his career. When they were in San Francisco one year, he threw a fit in the hotel room because she had talked "entirely too friendly" to some guy in the bar while she waited for him to come back from a business meeting. He was so furious then that she spent the whole of the night sitting up in an armchair, believing her marriage was over, and wondering how she would cope with three small children. Events like that had populated all the years and venues of their married life, intruding upon the good times like a chronic disease erupting out of remission, and now that they flooded her brain again like a fugue, she was astounded by how many times she could recall her silent rage.

She throws back the eiderdown in vehement dismissal of the kaleidoscope accosting her mind, and goes to the bathroom, then makes the bed. The effort exhausts her and she sinks into the chaise lounge where she often sits to read while waiting up for Noah. She gazes at the silver-framed family picture on the side table. An ideal family, everyone thinks so. One girl, two boys, all doing fine in school and never in any trouble, Noah a great success in business, herself active, self-determined.

They are, Noah and she, viewed as a strong, viable couple. (Only last week Jim Buchanan said to her, "I've looked long and hard for a model to follow. There just don't seem to be any good relationships . . . outside of you and Noah, of course.") In many respects, their marriage does work. Noah and she share similar interests and political views, like the same people for the most part, are known for being able to tease each other, although a keen observer would notice that usually it's Noah who teases her, mostly about her "socialist" convictions, her dedication to causes, as he calls it.

"Yeah, well, you know my wife," he says at parties, "always on the side of the underdog!"

Then, invariably, another husband tries to goad her into a reaction on some topical issue until, the center of attention, perspiration staining the underarms of her cocktail dress, she tries to explain the liberal position. After a while, she refuses the bait, excuses herself for a drink or a visit to the powder room. Once, another wife whispers to her, "Keep up the fight!"

But these episodes, and Noah's teasing, have begun to grate on her. The world's pain is no laughing matter, and her work is important. It's helped shape who she is, and that, of course, is part of the problem.

She gets up from the chaise lounge, grabs a clean towel from the bathroom closet, turns on the shower. The steam and the nettles of hot water sting her back and breasts like a therapeutic massage. She stands under the water for a long time, thinking again of the eighteen years she has shared with Noah.

The early years were unmarked by the kind of strains that have begun to chip away at them recently. But then, things were so different. Noah had just finished his MBA and was in a frenzy of work. The children, three in five years, dominated her time. It wasn't until they were in school that she began to realize how strangely exhausted she was, how anxious when she contemplated the future. Yet, from that void, that empty space of her soul that no one would have guessed was there, she gradually, privately, resurrected herself.

"I feel as though I'm drowning." She remembers saying that to Noah one night, after the kids were asleep. "Like I can't breathe."

Noah had put his arm around her. "You need an outlet, something to occupy yourself," he said gently.

But once she'd found a sitter and gone to work at the county hospital, he complained about late meals, and said things like, "Can we manage to get some clean socks around here?" when the laundry wasn't done. So she quit. And wondered why, suddenly, her libido had died.

Dr. Bowers said, "Theo, I've known you a long time. There's not a thing wrong with you that putting your mind to something wouldn't cure."

That was curiously unhelpful advice, and it made her angry because it was so dismissive, but she remembered it when she heard the radio ad for Mt. Saint Mary's Women's College a few weeks later.

"We're looking for the mature woman with life experience and a quest for knowledge!" the ad bellowed cheerfully. Why not, she thought, phoning the same day. Two weeks later she was enrolled.

She turns off the water and wraps herself in a fluffy towel, drying vigorously, then ties a terry robe around her. In the kitchen, she makes a pot of coffee and puts an English muffin in the toaster oven. She loves this kitchen. The whole house, really. Noah and she planned every aspect of it, every nuance, for ten years before they could afford to build it. From the window seat in the kitchen to the California room off the den to the deep fireplace in the sitting room, everything was planned for light and space and warmth. Why then, nearly eight years later, does she sit here feeling so confined and so oddly cold?

The years she spent as a returning college student changed her the most, she thinks, stirring her coffee and nibbling on the muffin. Those were the years when she absorbed everything new and challenging with hungry passion. She would study long into the night, often getting out of bed again after Noah had fallen asleep. Sometimes she contemplated things that frightened her, like the writings of Plath and Sexton and Woolf and Rich. She watched the younger women students, so self-assured, while she floundered and felt lost. But what influenced her most was the friendships with women like herself, the mid-life marrieds, so intent on examining their interior lives and giving voice to what was real for them.

Most were still good friends. Louise and Peggy and she had formed the women's group that meets monthly, still. What a joy it is to come together, sharing the pain and pleasure of their lives, being affirmed when an act of courage at home or at work is called for.

Noah never can quite understand.

"What the hell do you women DO there for three hours?" he asks whenever she says it's group night. He used to be openly jealous. "I don't know what you girls are up to," he would say then, "but I sure wish you wanted to be with me as much as you like to be with them." The emphasis always on "them," as if they were a secret society.

To his credit, Noah has come a long way, she thinks. He's learned a lot about the issues that hold her attention. And he has definitely lightened up. When she was in graduate school, and then when she got the job at the mayor's office, he boasted about her success, and stopped complaining so much about things at home. But still, there was the undercurrent.

And it's the undercurrent that's begun to suffocate her now, to siphon her energy, to make her feel sometimes that in order to save herself she will have to let go, give way to the undertow, swirl into the black hole and let the chaos consume her, emerging wherever the tumult deposits her. These thoughts inflame the secret spaces of her mind more often now, triggered, it seems, by a kind of latent rage whenever she remembers Noah's control and quiet manipulation over the years. For a long time, because they were so terrifying, she managed to push such ideas aside whenever they intruded. But it's grown increasingly difficult for her to deny the subtle sensations of longing and of sadness which pervade her being lately, and last night the storm clouds broke with hurricane force, pulling her down again into the abyss and closer to the trench of action.

She rises from the kitchen table, wipes the crumbs into the palm of her hand, swallows the last of the tepid coffee. Hugging her robe, she mounts the stairs, puts on jeans and a white T-shirt, grabs a cardigan, runs a brush through her hair, and sets out for a brisk walk.

The party last night was one neither of them wanted to attend. "Just consider it overtime," Noah said when they were dressing.

These obligatory entertainments seem to have shaped the whole of their social life, she thinks. Everyone agrees they're loathsome events, but no one risks changing the pattern, and whenever she suggests that they not host one, Noah says, "But we have to. A lot of business gets done."

It was a wonderful surprise, though, to come upon Philip Warren plucking hors d'oeuvres off a silver tray. She hadn't seen him since graduate school when he taught Organizational Psychology and supervised her field study. His wife died that year, and they had become friends. She would find him gazing blankly out the window, and then he would talk, haltingly, about her. Gradually, their conversation began to include other things, growing into firm friendship. Noah, of course, couldn't understand why she "spent so much time" with Philip, or why in the world she included him in some of their dinner parties until he retired from the university. He thought it a suspicious and unlikely relationship. "After all," he would say, "he's rather old to be hanging around you all the time, isn't he?"

"How terrific to see you!" Philip says, grabbing her arm, when he realizes it is her. "I've missed you!"

They embrace. She has missed him too. She asks how he is, what he is doing at the party.

"I'm relocating back as a consultant," he tells her. Coopted by Big Business in his retirement, he says, rolling his eyes and winking.

Later, when they are undressing, Noah refuses to speak, retreating into the icy zone he inhabits when he's angry with her. She asks what is wrong.

He says nothing. Then he says, "Unless you've been seeing that Warren fellow."

She stares at him as though he were a creature from another planet.

"Well, you did seem to be sucking up to him tonight, don't you think?" he says.

"I wasn't 'sucking up' to him, or anyone else for that matter, Noah," she says. "He's my friend. I was glad to see him again."

"Glad is one thing, Theo. I think you were being unduly familiar." He speaks those words as if they were strangers, a grown adult addressing an errant child.

If the feeling inside her stomach at that moment could metamorphose into animated life, she thinks, she will give birth to a fire-breathing, scaly, sharp-toothed, odious monster. Then she will watch her offspring, conceived in rage and psychic violence, devour its father.

"Do you know, Noah, I used to be afraid of you," she says. "Not in a physical way, of course. I don't mean that. But I used to think that whatever you told me to do I had to do, like a good girl, so that I could get to stay here . . . "

"Theo . . . "

"Stay here in my own life."

"For chrissakes, Theo, you don't need to go off on some psychoshit." His eyes have that translucent look they get when he is furious.

Something takes hold of her then, something that makes her feel very powerful. "Let me just be clear about something, Noah," she says then. "I am an adult. I get to choose my friends. I decide who they are, how much time I spend with them, what we do, and what we say to each other. Got that?"

"I don't ask much," Noah hisses. "Just a little give and take now and again. God knows, I've supported you when you needed it. You'd have to admit that, wouldn't you?"

"Yes. You've been absolutely splendid," she concedes, cynically at first, and then with care. "You've been a good husband most of the time, and a great father."

"What then, Theo?" He looks truly bewildered, hurt.

"Noah, you bleed me," she says. "I'm spiritually anemic with all the do's and don'ts of our lives. The rules and rituals, the keeping up appearances. The obligations. Always doing The Right Thing so that people — or you — don't get The Wrong Impression."

He looks at her, wounded and confused. She goes on. "Everything I love — to be, to do, to share with people — somehow you weaken, turn to pain for me. I know you don't mean to do it. But most of the time, I creep around inside myself, trying to keep the peace, feeling less and less able to breathe the air I need to stay alive."

"God, Theo, all I asked was . . ."

"I know what you're asking, Noah. I know it like I've never known before."

"Theo, for God's sake, what's happening to you? It's like you're someone else . . . ."

"Yes. I suppose that's exactly what it's like."

They go to bed shortly afterward, each clinging to the far shores of the king-sized sea they share. During the night, Noah inches toward her until his back rests against her side. In the early morning, he dresses quietly for work, assuming they have somehow cleared the air. The children, like everyone else in their intimate community, arise to greet the new day with no reason to suspect that anything is amiss.

But Theo Maizel is alert in a way she has never quite been before. She has seen the dark side of her marriage, and for better or for worse, she knows she has crossed irrevocably in the night into its shadow, and that the surrounding grayness will change her life from this moment forward, and forever.

GERT

✦ ◇ ✦

The Incident

Wow, Grandma!" Timmy's blue eyes open wide at the sight of his disheveled grandmother on the front porch. "You look like you've been to the wars!" he gasps, imitating her response to him whenever he comes home from playing, scruffy and with skinned knees.

"Well, dear, I've had a bit of a scrape up. But not to worry. Everything is fine." Gert adjusts the printed scarf tied loosely around her neck and smooths the front of her jersey and slacks. Then she runs a futile hand over her thinning gray hair and wipes the dust from her eyelids.

"Timmy! Is that Grandma?"

"Yeah! And you should see her!" It is then that Timmy notices the car. "Hey. What happened to your car?" he squeals.

"Well, let's just say there's been an incident . . ."

"An accident? Mother, have you had an accident? Haven't I been saying you should give up driving? Really, Mother . . . " Judy descends the hall stairs clutching a dustcloth, her eyes wide, nostrils flared with admonition.

"Can you all just stay quite calm," Gert says, passing from the screen door toward the kitchen. "I wouldn't have come here at all except that you were so close. And I couldn't think for a minute where to tell the police to come, so I just said to come here."

"The police! Mother, what on earth . . . ? There's been an accident, hasn't there?"

"No, Judy, not an accident. An incident. Do, for

116

heaven's sake, be calm. I'll tell you about it when the policeman arrives, but right now, I want a cup of tea."

Gert has lived in the United States for nearly forty-five years, but still, she craves a cup of tea, and speaks in her clipped and cultivated British accent when she is the least bit tense.

In the kitchen, busying herself with the tea kettle, she begins to feel the color returning to her face.

"So Grandma, what happened? Tell me!"

"Timmy! Be quiet. Can't you see that Grandma's in a state?"

"Judy, dear, no one is in a state, as you put it, but you and Timmy."

"Look, Mother, I'm sorry, but this sort of thing has got to stop. If it's not one thing, it's another with you and that car. First, you get a speeding ticket on the interstate, then you're fined for emission control, and now, not one week later, you're involved in an accident. It's high time, I've told you, that you stop driving. It's ludicrous at your age, that flashy red sports car, anyway."

"It was not an accident, Judy. It was an incident. Let us be very clear. And," she sips her tea, "it's not a sports car. It's a hatchback. Furthermore, I will thank you not to lecture me. I am not a child." She looks at her daughter above the teacup rim. "Besides, as I've always told you, age is a state of mind. Nothing more."

Judy rolls her eyes and raises a coffee mug to her pursed lips. For a moment, mother and daughter stare at each other in silent frustration. Then Judy's face softens and Gert sees in her daughter's features a hint of her American father as he looked in 1946 when they married. My, but he was handsome in his uniform! Gert had gone quite balmy over him in the canteen in London when he teased her about her accent. "Oh, go on, you're a regular Charlie," she had said.

"Hey, how'd you know my name?" he asked then, with mock surprise.

"You're all Charlies, aren't you?"

And from that day on, till death tore them apart nearly forty years later, she had called him "Charlie," even though his real name was Everett James Teal.

At the knock on the screen door, Judy jumps, spilling her coffee on the counter. "I'll get it!" Timmy says. Gert puts her teacup gently back on the saucer. All three of them make their way to the front door.

"Morning, Ma'am. Officer Boren," the policeman says, flashing his badge at Judy, who opens the door and ushers him in gravely. "Hello, Officer," Gert says, smiling. "Won't you have a seat?"

"Thank you, Mrs. Teal." He settles into the easy chair across from the sofa and pulls out a notepad. "Now, maybe you can tell me exactly what happened, I mean in more detail than what you said at the scene."

At the word "scene," Judy cringes. "I've been telling my mother that she really ought to give up driving. I mean, at her age . . . "

The officer looks at her quizzically, then at Gert, who has seated herself comfortably on the sofa across from him, Timmy by her side.

"Well," she begins, "as I said to you before, I was driving up Elm toward Main this morning, on my way to my exercise class, when this rather seedy car pulled up quite close behind. At first, I didn't think too much of it, just a couple of youths driving poorly, I thought. Then, out of the clear blue, they rammed me! I mean, can you believe it?"

Judy begins to speak, but Gert, seeing her poised, cuts her off.

"Well, naturally, I stopped, to get the particulars, and that's when they approached me and said it was a hold-up. Well, that's not actually what they said. One of them just told me to hand over my purse, 'or I'd be sorry,' is what he said."

"Wow!" Timmy interjects. "The neatest things happen to you, Grandma!"

"Now I wasn't going to just hand over my purse, was I?

I mean, what next? And as I was in my car and they weren't, I thought I'd just slip away from them. So I put my foot on the gas and took off."

"You what?" Judy jumps up and paces across the living room to the fireplace.

"I took off, dear. Unfortunately, I suppose since I was driving shift and they weren't, they were able to catch up with me. And that was rather unfortunate because that meant I had to outsmart them to get away, and they were really quite angry with me. So I did something I probably shouldn't have done. I drove onto a few lawns and tried to go down the alley, you know, that little bit of alley off Elm Street, only when they chased me I sort of hit the wall . . . "

"You what! Good God, Mother!"

" . . . and that turned me around so that I was in the ridiculous position of being in pursuit of them!" With that, Gert breaks into a broad grin, then a spout of laughter. "Can you imagine it, Judy? It was like a French farce!"

Judy looks at the officer as if together they should consider committing Gert. Officer Boren, lowering his eyes and fiddling with his notepad, tries to restrain a smile. Timmy says, for the third time that morning, "Wow!"

"Well, then," Gert continues, relishing now the continuation of her monologue, "I chased them back into the street. I mean, one can't allow that sort to just get away with it, can one?" She pauses to gauge the response to her rhetorical question, and when there is none, she goes on. "By then, of course, there was a great brouhaha, with people running out of their houses as if they were all on fire. I tell you, it was a right carry on! And someone had called the police, so when we approached Main, well there they were like a sort of road block and the poor blokes were absolutely trapped and, well, Officer, you know the rest, don't you?"

Gert looks at her audience. Judy has never looked quite so nonplussed. Officer Boren is smiling and shaking his head. Timmy, speechless, bounces imperceptibly on the sofa and beams at his Grandma Gert.

"I simply must have another cup of tea," Gert says when Officer Boren has gone. "And, actually, I wouldn't mind a biscuit." She is now quite flushed, having been the center of attention for the last half hour, and she likes the silence that has overtaken Judy for the moment, however short-lived.

"Mother, do you realize what might have happened to you? You could have been seriously hurt, even killed. It was totally irresponsible. You are no spring chicken and you have no business acting as if you were."

"Wonder Woman!" Timmy yells, flying through the kitchen with a model of Superman about to be cata-pulted out of his left hand.

"You lacked all judgment . . . " Judy drones on.

Gert watches her passively, without listening. How had Judy, the love child of herself and Charlie, turned out to be so austere, so fearful, so lacking in humor and vitality? Even as a child she had been dull, and she was dull still. Charlie used to say, whenever she pouted or took things too seriously, that she'd inherited her personality from Gert's family, her good looks from his, and Gert thinks now that there might well have been some truth to it. For a while, when Judy was in college, it looked as though she might learn to lighten up after all. But when she married Bob, solid, self-righteous, boring Bob, her early potential for negativism had solidified as if she'd been biblically turned to salt. And that seemed to be that.

"Oh, Judy, do stop preaching. It's ever so boring," Gert says, retrieving the words from the recesses of her uncon-scious mind. "You really must learn not to go on so," she says then, maternally.

Suddenly, she feels weary of her daughter, as weary as she had in the days of her infancy when there was no true rest, no freedom. She often felt suffocated then, and she feels it now.

"I must go," she says. "There's so much to do. I have to call the insurance and the auto shop. And I could do with a bath. I don't want to miss my dinner engagement tonight either."

"Why don't you stay in and rest? You've had a shock . . . "

But Gert is already on her way to the front door. What would Judy think, she wonders, bemused, if she knew that my "dinner engagement" was actually a date with my new bridge partner? She smiles as Timmy comes up and nestles his head in her fleshy stomach as he hugs her hips. "I love you, Grandma."

"And I love you! You're my special boy." She pats his blond head. "And one of these days, just as soon as my car is fixed, we're going to have an outing, aren't we? Maybe we'll go fishing over at the river. What do you say to that?"

"Wow!" he says, caught again in the monosyllable of affection and awe he reserves for his grandmother.

Gert reaches out to hug Judy, and in a clash of sudden, intense emotions that overtake her like an unexpected squall, she holds her only child intensely to her breast. It is a terrible thing, she thinks, to dislike your own child, to wish her other than she is, to feel amidst abiding devotion and the deepest of love bonds a distance which can never be breached, and which renders you the loneliest moments of your life. Then she kisses her daughter lingeringly on the cheek.

"Try to be happy, my darling. Do try. If only I could make you understand . . . "

Judy pulls back and looks at her mother with misty puzzlement.

"Never mind," Gert says with a sigh, gathering up her purse and keys with renewed energy. "Walk me to the car, then, there's a love."

Gert backs out of the driveway, waves to Timmy and blows a kiss to Judy, who is somber but somehow softer than she had been in the kitchen. Judy waves back and pulls her cardigan around her shoulders. It is an odd gesture of age on such a warm day, and it is not lost on Gert, who removes her scarf, adjusts her rearview mirror, and heads home.

ROSIE

✦ ✧ ✦

Rosie's Tape

You have a choice," she always said. It was her trademark phrase, and I hear it now, playing in my head like a tape recorder with a stuck off button. She said it about everything. "You have a choice," she would say to a stubborn rosebush. "You can either open up and smile in my garden, or you can shrivel up and die." Once I heard her say it to a centipede. "You can get along out of my way, or you can meet your maker at the end of my broomstick." When I was three years old and whined, "I don't know what to call you. Are you Rosie, or are you my Grandma?" she answered, "You call me whatever you want. It's your choice." So I called her Grandma Rosie, which seemed to please her. She always did like an original solution to a problem.

Grandma Rosie's ideas about choice went beyond bugs and rosebushes. She was fierce — even vehement — about anyone or anything that violated a person's right to decide. "Imagine!" she exclaimed when the community went crazy about certain books in the library. "Do they think people haven't the right to decide themselves about Mark Twain and Mr. Salinger?" And when *Roe v. Wade* gave women the right to abortion, "Well, it's about time, that's all I can say." Strong stuff from a woman with an eighth grade education who never got much beyond Pennsylvania, except in her vivid and active imagination.

By the time my mother grew up, her version of Rosie's tape came out more like this: It's my right and it's my business. But her tape played inaudibly. She just went about her business with conviction, never looking back. When she decided to drop out of school to get a job in

New York, she didn't ask anyone for permission or advice. She just announced one day that that was what she was going to do. And when she'd saved up $700, she just up and left and never looked back with any regret, even though she ended up going back to college years later while she was working and raising two kids.

So choice, deciding exactly how we would live, from the mundane to the most monumental of issues, has been a tradition — a religion, my father always said — for the women of my Grandma Rosie's lineage. Our tenacity in that regard has served each of us well.

I first began to suspect trouble more than a year ago, when she couldn't remember whether or not she had taken her insulin in the morning. "Isn't that funny," she'd say. "I just can't seem to recall." Then there were other things she couldn't call up in her mind. A familiar date, someone's name, where she had put her purse or the latest book she was trying to read but could not finish because she couldn't remember where she had left off. I got scared that she would go into diabetic shock and felt unnerved by her forgetfulness, so one day I suggested she ought to get a good check-up. "It's up to you, of course," I said, anticipating her resistance. "But if I were you, Grandma Rosie, I'd get a top-to-toe, just to keep yourself in such good shape." To my surprise, she didn't resist. And to my growing angst, when I came to fetch her for the doctor's appointment two weeks later, she was sitting in her armchair staring into space. "Oh, were we supposed to go somewhere, dear?"

I guess from the first I'd worried about Alzheimer's, pushing it away from my conscious mind like a mother who refuses to think of an auto accident when her teenager is late home. So I wasn't shocked when the doctor called me into his office a few weeks after Rosie's tests were completed. Only horrified. "Your grandmother has probably had the disease since her late forties," he said sympathetically but with the directness he knew I desired. "She is having a sudden exacerbation, and frankly, from what you've told me, and from her response to testing, I think we're going to see a fairly rapid progression. Very soon now, she's going to need constant care. You should begin to look into nursing homes."

The thought of my Grandma Rosie, feisty, energetic, political, fun-loving Rosie, shuffling up and down a nursing home corridor, making paper flowers at Easter and Styrofoam Christmas decorations in December, being called "Dear" and "Sweetie" by people who meant well but had no right to be intimate or patronizing, was more than I could take. "I can't let it come to that," I said, fighting back the panicky outburst on the edge of my eyes.

I started going over to Rosie's every day then, in the morning before work to supervise her giving herself insulin which I had drawn up into the syringe, and in the evening to make sure she ate and was settled for the night. After a while, I had to get a visiting nurse and Meals on Wheels and a neighbor to help. But we made it for a few months like that.

I could never decide which was worse, spending time with Grandma Rosie when she was lucid, or when she was in such a disoriented fog that she seemed like a stranger, a foreigner who had just dropped in from nowhere, and whose language and culture were completely unknown to me. Either way I knew I was losing her, and in her moments of clarity, she knew it too. "Something's very wrong," she would say, looking me in the eye more directly and fiercely than I had ever known her to do. "I don't know what it is, but something is not right in my head. When it comes over me, I feel lost, and I don't like that. Don't like being out of control." One night, she said something even more to the point. "I want you to promise me something, Darcy," she said, and that's when she looked at me so piercingly. "I want you to promise me

that you will never — never, never! — let me be foolish or
out of control or useless. I am trusting you with something very precious to me, and that is my dignity. I think I
care more about dignity than anything else, really. Do
you understand what I am saying?"

I understood perfectly. It was something she and I had
talked about like two friends after my mother died. We
both held the same passionate conviction that my mother
should have put a stop to her treatment before it rav-
ished her more than the cancer. And we both knew she
would have if she had not gone so far with things that the
choice was no longer hers. "Timing is everything," Rosie
had said then. "Especially when it comes to making
choices in life."

In a way it was timing that made me finally break down
and take the next step. The very week that Carriage Hill
Convalescent Center called to say Rosie's name had
reached the top of the waiting list was the week she
assaulted the visiting nurse when she tried to inject her.
"And who the hell does she think she is, the bitch?" she
raged at me uncharacteristically when I asked her about
it. Her outbursts were becoming more frequent, and
more generalized, so I waited several days before bring-
ing up Carriage Hill. Then, "You know, Grandma Rosie, I
think it would be a good idea for you to consider, just for
a week or two, spending some time over at that Senior
Center where Mrs. Cambridge lives. I understand in the
summer they do a lot of things, like theater parties and
stuff. That would be nice for you while I'm on vacation.
Think it over." A few days later she said, "You know that
place, what's it called, where Mrs. You-Know is? Well, just
while you're away, I'll visit. But as soon as you're back,
I'm out of there. Understand?" I understood all too well.
Grandma Rosie was afraid now.

She went amiably, thank God, as though it were an outing. Mrs. Cambridge's daughter went with us, and when

we got there the staff gave a little tea party for all of us, Mrs. Cambridge presiding as if it were a major social event. I suppose for her it was. I kept up a good front until I left, and then shattered like a china vase that had been flung violently against a brick wall. The nurse told me when I phoned that night that Rosie was quiet but fine, and seemed to have enjoyed the day.

I didn't really go on vacation, but I stayed away from the home for a week to see how Rosie would do. Every time I called, they told me she was "quiet" or "doing just fine." It wasn't until I went in the second week that I saw for myself what was really happening to my grandmother.

She was sitting in a chair when I entered her room with a large bouquet of flowers in my hand. Her thinning gray hair was brushed severely back from her face instead of in its usual chaotic heap on her forehead. She was dressed in a clean striped blouse and a plaid skirt, creating a jumble of color that assaulted her own good taste in clothes, and worst of all, she had on knee-highs instead of proper stockings, and slippers. She stared straight at the flowers in my hand, and clear through me. "Hi, Grandma Rosie!" I managed. No response. "I'm back." Nothing. "She's been like that all day, dear," a nurse said, coming up behind me. "Not to worry. She'll be herself again once she gets used to things here." A sickening feeling of hot bile crept up my stomach and into my throat.

"Can I see the head nurse?" I asked. "I'd like to review what's been happening this week." I moved toward the nursing station without waiting for a reply. No one was there. I looked at the charts hanging alphabetically on the carousel. "It's your choice," I heard Rosie's tape saying to me with comic irony as I lifted hers from the rack. "Patient depressed. Not eating. Exhibiting signs of psychosis (catatonia). Psychiatrist called. 25 mg. Melaril ordered, q.i.d."

My head swam. Here it was, happening before my eyes. Everything she had feared, I had dreaded. No. No, no, no!

I put the chart back just as an aide approached the station. "Can I help you?" "Yes. I was just looking for a vase, actually."

Rosie never spoke to me the whole time I was there. I busied myself arranging the flowers, which now seemed a mockery, and making small talk. All the while I felt her anger like ice on the back of my neck.

A few days later, before I even had a chance to think what to do, the call came. "This is Donna, the nurse on 2 East. Don't be alarmed, but I thought you should know. Your grandmother made something of a suicide gesture last night. She didn't hurt herself. It was really just to get attention. But we thought you should know. She wrapped the nurses' bell cord around her neck, several times. She was actually pulling on it when we found her. Of course, we've called the psychiatrist."

"No!"

"Excuse me?"

"No psychiatrist. No more punishment. That was not the act of a crazy person. That was a gesture of utter sanity. My grandmother is in abject despair and she is trying to let you know. She is trapped! Physically and mentally trapped. Everything is gone, even her dignity. Can't you see? Don't do a thing until I get there."

I poured myself a drink and tried to calm down. For the first time in six years I longed for a cigarette. What to do? What to do, not to break my promise to Rosie?

When I got to the nursing home, I asked once again for the head nurse. "Clarence," the aide called out to my surprise. "Someone wants to see you. A relative." Clarence emerged from one of the rooms, hands in rubber gloves. His broad African face was kind. "What can I do for you?" he asked in the lilting accent of Nigeria.

"I want to ask you a question," I said. "It's just between you and me. Understand?" He didn't, of course, but he nodded assent just the same. "What would happen if my grandmother were to say she didn't want to take her insulin shots anymore? I mean, I know what would happen, but would you honor that wish?"

Clarence's eyes grew wide and quizzical. His expression was poised between shock and a smile. It was the face of someone when you have said to them "Would it be all right for me to kill my grandmother?" "This is a very strange question," he said. "Why would you . . . It would be . . . "

"Yes, I know," I said. "I know exactly what I am saying, but would you honor it if she said 'stop'?"

"Yes, we would honor it."

"Thank you. And remember, this is just between you and me, yes?"

"You mean you don't want me to write it down in the chart?" he asked with the hint of a gentle grin. And in that moment I blessed him for his connection, his humanity, his reverence for life. "Tell me, Clarence," I said, turning toward Grandma Rosie's room. "What do you do in your country, you who revere old age so much? How do you help your people pass peacefully into the night?"

"Well, we don't have institutions like this for a start," he said, looking at me again with a kind of empathy for which I will be forever grateful.

When I went back to Rosie's room, she was lying in bed, staring straight up at the ceiling, motionless. I took her hand, cherishing its warmth as I had done when I was a child. She squeezed my hand, then grimaced. A tear slid down toward her ear. "I love you so much, Grandma Rosie," I said. Then, "You know, you could say you don't want your insulin. They can't force you. It's your choice. Or you could say you don't want to eat. No one will make you. It's up to you. Do you understand what I'm telling you?"

"So then what would happen," she asked, child-like.

"You'd pass away."

"So who would make all the arrangements?" I wanted to laugh. Grandma Rosie. Ever the organizer.

"I'll take care of everything. You don't need to worry." She squeezed my hand again.

I come every day now. She is usually in bed, eyes closed or staring at the ceiling. When I take her hand it is always warm and she squeezes mine so I think she still knows who I am. And every day I tell her again. "You could say you don't want your insulin. It's up to you. It's your choice." I don't know whether the tape plays for her as it so often does for me. Maybe in spite of herself, she is too tenacious about life. She told me once, after the bell cord episode, that she didn't really want to commit suicide, she just wanted the pain to be gone. Maybe she forgets before she has time to tell them. But somehow, reminding her is my way of giving back her gift to me. When I sit here with her, squeezing her hand, I think she knows, and that is something that makes both of us feel better. And when the time finally comes, however it happens, it will be good to think that in the end, it was Grandma Rosie's choice.

ALICIA
✦ ◇ ✦
Khartoum Nights

The thing about Khartoum is the heat. It wraps itself around you like Saran Wrap the minute you step off the plane and it never lets up, not even at night. It smothers and oppresses — a heavy blanket that won't lift no matter how much you squirm to kick it off. It makes you feel like gasping for air sometimes, like you want to move and be still at the same time, like you'll die without a shower and a set of clean underwear.

I suppose that was the reason I first noticed her. She seemed so cool, so dry, so unperturbed. She shuffled across the linoleum floor of the hotel as I guzzled two Cokes, one after the other, the night I arrived, and the sight of her made me sad. Surely she wasn't transient like the rest of us who stayed at the run-down Athenum, counting the days until we could leave, because it had the only reliable telex in all of Khartoum.

I'd gone down on a UN assignment and was glad it was only a ten-day stint. Khartoum was hardly my idea of an exotic work destination, and I thought the project unlikely in view of the pervasive political tension. Jack, my colleague, had convinced me the Athenum was the place to stay, despite its seedy appearance.

"You don't want to be in the Hilton!" he'd bellowed on the phone. "All the real people stay here. It's not the lap of luxury, but it's where all the action is!"

He was right about that. The small hotel teemed with activity day and night, especially night. Most of the foreign journalists stayed there along with aid workers and missionaries in transit. Run by a Greek family long resident in the Sudan, it was spare but adequate and the food was plentiful and reasonably good, considering the setting. Before long, everyone sort of knew each other and in the evening, sitting in the sparse lobby clinging to badly needed liquid refreshment, it was like coming home to family. When the evening meal was ready, we were summoned communally into the small dining room by the family matriarch where, seated in our regular places, three or four familiar waiters served up the night's offering, always the same soup and hearty meat-and-potato stew followed by a custard-covered sweet. Then, back to the lobby for coffee and perhaps a liqueur before retiring to our monastic bedrooms and shared bath.

Khartoum was the most impoverished place I'd ever seen. Men, lean with hunger and lack of work, languished in the dusty streets without hope, white cotton caftan shirts fluttering limply in the slim breeze. Somnolent dogs, their ribs and tongues sticking out, scavenged for bits of food. Children cried inconsolably. Women passed each other resolutely without looking into the other's eyes. Even at university and government offices, people seemed to move in slow motion, as if imminently they would all collapse in a chorus of heat prostration. The Athenum was a veritable oasis in the midst of such silent misery, and only then because we knew that eventually, we could all get out.

But she couldn't get out. That was clear from the beginning. And so I became obsessed with knowing who she was, and how she came to be there, wandering the hotel lobby for what seemed all eternity, in her black polka-dot dress, her felt slippers, her nylons knotted at the knees, and her tattered black plastic purse, carried in knurled hands which still retained the elegance of earlier days. Thin wisps of white hair held back in a drooping French twist by a few black hairpins framed a face now lined, but hosting the remnants of classic beauty, especially around the gray-blue pools of her eyes. Those eyes. They haunt me still when I remember her.

I thought then, and I still do when I look back on it, that we'd made contact with our eyes. At first, embarrassed by her solitude, afraid somehow that her situation would encroach upon me and keep me prisoner in that place of no air and trickling sweat down my back, I only smiled politely and averted my eyes. The conditions of her confinement were private, I convinced myself. But then, gradually, bravely, with mutually reinforced courage, we began to hold each other's gaze, in an odd sort of trust and friendship. I would be sitting with Jack, clutching my Coke bottle and pressing it's wet coldness against my neck and forehead, maybe talking with the Belgian journalist who was just back from Addas or just about to take off for Eritrea, and she would appear like an apparition, dignified and quiet in . . . what? Madness? Despair?

One day, finally, I asked Jack, in a kind of rhetorical reflection, what he knew of her. He said he had asked the Greek once, but had only learned that her name was Alicia and she lived in the hotel at the will and mercy of her son, a businessman, who traveled all over the world and only came to visit once a year or so. No one seemed to know, really, how or why she had come to spend her last lonely days in this godforsaken corner of the world, or quite what she had been in life before entering limbo.

I began to look forward to seeing her, to knowing that she had survived another night, to smiling at her, and exchanging imperceptible nods. In an odd sort of way, I began to feel an extraordinary connection to her. She anchored me and made me feel safe when the oppression of Khartoum nights made me panicky. I imagined that one time very soon we would sit together in the humid lobby, quiet and conspiratorial, trading girl talk and revealing ourselves in deep understanding across the abyss of age and circumstance which divided us forever. I almost had the sense that we were each planning such a rendezvous, savoring the moment when we would finally sip tea together and share the secrets of our lives. But we continued instead to nod and smile and like each other with our eyes.

Once, when I was talking to the missionary mother and her two daughters, sallow, skinny children who looked in desperate need of crisp New England air, my silent friend passed by, lingering for a moment as if beckoning me to come with her. I had a deep urge to excuse myself, to rise from the plastic chair stuck to my back, to put my arm around her frail shoulder and say, "Yes! Yes, let's do sit and talk now," but I didn't do that. I only gave her a half smile and later regretted not excusing myself from the missionary as I tossed on my slender, hard pallet and willed the ceiling fan to move faster.

I'm not sure, looking back now, what kept me from reaching out to her, but I think it had to do with not wishing to open up her pain. Also, I was loath to intrude upon her dignity, or to give her something (friendship, hope?) which in a few days would disappear with me on an airplane, to make her uncomfortable or embarrassed in any way. I was also timid, I suppose, because everyone else thought her slightly crazy and I didn't know what would be unleashed if I opened the floodgates, although I am ashamed now to confess that.

At any rate, at the end of my ten working days, I escaped into the night aboard a Luftansa flight to Cairo, and civilization, and I never saw her again.

I did phone Jack to ask about her, however, about two weeks later, when I read in the paper that the Athenum had been bombed. Had he had any word, I wondered?

Yes, he said. He'd learned that two of the waiters and the missionary family had been killed instantly when the explosive was lobbed into the dining room. He didn't know about the Belgian journalist. No one seemed to have heard from him so they assumed he was still in the bush somewhere.

And my friend, I asked?

Jack said she was fine, she hadn't been in the vicinity of the bomb when it exploded, and as far as he knew, she was staying on at the hotel.

He'd gotten his information, Jack said, because as usual, the telex at the Athenum was working perfectly.

Somehow, that didn't surprise me any more than the newspaper report on the day I phoned, which recorded the fact that Khartoum had hit 110 degrees, with no relief in sight.

MOLLY
✦ ✧ ✦
Benchmarks

Molly sits down on the familiar bench and lets herself experience the physical relief and sheer pleasure of being back. It is like a homecoming. Even the pigeons seem excited, strutting around her feet like self-impressed headwaiters seeing to it that all is well at an important banquet. Molly smiles. "I know what you're after," she says, reaching for her black leather handbag. Carefully, she opens the gold clasp with the inlaid mother-of-pearl stone. The incongruity of the handsome purse with her worn and faded wool coat does not escape her. The handbag, a gift from her daughter Hannah, makes her feel wistful, even melancholy if she isn't careful. Maybe next year a new coat, Molly thinks. Reaching into the purse, she draws out a bag of bread crumbs and unties the knot she has carefully tied in the reused plastic bag. "Here you are, my friends," she says, scattering the crumbs around in a wide semicircle in front of her outstretched feet. "Enjoy!"

While she waits for Sam — and she is utterly sure he will come — Molly decides to reorganize her purse. She hasn't done this for a while. It will be interesting to rediscover its treasures. She decides to lay them neatly on the bench, to recategorize them before returning them to the handbag. Starting with larger items first, she places her plastic French wallet on the bench to her left. The slight tear in the corner of the change compartment is disconcerting. She will need to be careful not to let it get any worse, she notes. Before moving on, she pauses to look at the contents of the faded plastic card carrier. There are no credit cards. In the first pocket a library card and her social security card rest back to back. The next window reveals a pink square noting Molly's blood type, and whom to contact in a medical emergency on one side, and her voter registration on the other. The remaining windows showcase pictures of her daughter Hannah, with her children, a solitary picture of her late husband, whose uncanny resemblance to Harry Truman people always note, and a wrinkled photograph of her son, Isaac, just before he died, with his pudgy legs crossed and his head tilted in the classic pose of 1940s children's photography.

Next to the wallet, Molly places a plastic see-through case in the shape of a crescent moon with a zipper at the top. Inside the case are a square mirror with a tortoise-shell back, a worn lipstick, a small pink comb that looks brand new, and a crisp white linen handkerchief with frayed edges. To her right, Molly lays her neatly folded black veil which she uses on windy days to keep her hair in place, tying the triangle corners under her chin. Her solitary key comes next with its large wooden keychain in the shape of a heart, now devoid of paint because so many years have passed since Hannah's oldest gave it to her. Under this, so that it will not blow away, she lays the book review that she has clipped from the *New York Times* that morning. When she isn't so tired, she will go to the library. Maybe Sam will come with her.

Before replacing the contents in her purse, Molly feels around its bottom. There is a ballpoint pen, a crumpled receipt from Kresge's, on the back of which she has scribbled the doctor's phone number, and a small calendar-cum-address book which she has not had occasion to use for some weeks now. No need to lay them out on the bench. Meticulously, she returns the items to the purse, using the leather divider in it to separate the larger items from the small. When she has finished, she snaps the mother-of-pearl clasp gently shut, and places the hand-

bag securely in her lap. Then, clucking softly to the
pigeons, she sits back to wait for Sam.

They started coming to their bench nearly a year ago.
Inexplicably it was always free, as if pigeons and pedestri-
ans alike honored an invisible "Reserved" sign. Neither
of them questioned this. It was simply their bench after a
while. Sam usually arrived first, just as he had on the day
they first talked. Molly remembers that encounter in fine
detail. It had been a chilly day and, as she approached,
she saw him sitting there huddled and scowling mildly as
if deep in thought.

"Do you mind if I sit?" she had asked.

"It's a public park. Sit." Then, "Damn pigeons. Phffe!
Dirty. Carry disease."

"I suppose. But they like people." Then she scattered
bread crumbs on the side of the bench away from Sam
and, like a mother whose children are eating well, smiled
with satisfaction.

"You must be a regular, they should like you so much,"
Sam said, peering over the rim of his glasses. "Never saw
so many damn pigeons!"

"I hope I haven't disturbed you."

"It's a public park, so who can complain," he shrugged,
tipping his hat to her as he prepared to move on.

A week later, when Molly returned to the bench, he
was there again. "So, if it isn't Miss Regular. Where are
your friends today?"

"I didn't bring any bread. I don't think they'll bother you."

"God forbid they should starve because of me!"

"Oh, I wouldn't worry about that! I only feed them
sometimes. I started doing it when my granddaughter was
little. She used to come to visit and she liked feeding them.
It sort of got me in the habit. I come to the park a lot," she
said almost apologetically.

"Me too. My son — he's a CPA in Passaic — he says to
me, 'Pop, you're not dead yet. Get some exercise. Take an

interest in things.' So I come to the park, he shouldn't think I'm not interested. Truth of the matter is, I'm not interested. But sitting outside is better than sitting inside. If you know what I mean."

Molly knew. For her the park was a sanctuary, an escape from the one-room apartment that imprisoned her for so many hours of her day. Outside of her errands and her visits to the library — and an occasional visitor — her life was one of solitude. In many ways, she had chosen this life, refusing to move closer to Hannah and the grandchildren. It wasn't just that she didn't want to be a burden. She remembered life when it had been frenetic, even when there was only one child. Working in Sidney's jewelry shop to help make ends meet, taking care of the children, writing a little poetry when there was time, and finally giving up after Isaac died. At first she had relished the quietude of her own space, even tried to write again. But loneliness had crept up on her. She couldn't remember exactly when. By the time it enveloped her, it was too late to ask Hannah if she could come.

She and Sam never talk about these things. They only exchange facts. But she is intuitive enough to understand that his cynicism stems from a deep and terrifying loneliness. She finds him pathetically comic most of the time.

And more and more, she, like he, has come to look forward to the bench visits, which have begun to occur more frequently and to last longer. Gradually, when there are fewer facts to share, and she knows about his life as a tailor, and later a government clerk, and his wife, Paula, and their son, Phil, and the disappointments and the few joys, they begin to talk about politics and books. Politics is his domain, and he pontificates with impressive oratory about the flaws of every administration since FDR. Books are hers, and she tells him about the classics with all the passion of Mary Pickford once she gets on the subject.

And then suddenly, the fever and the pain in her spine, and she isn't there anymore. Weeks pass. "It'll be all right," the doctor says. "It just takes time. But you mustn't go up and down the steps yet. Is there someone who can help you?"

"Yes, Mrs. Nullen can come." But she never asks her to go to the bench to tell him.

"What about your friend?" Mrs. Nullen asks.

"I wouldn't want to worry him," she says. And I wouldn't want him to see this place, she thinks.

Then, finally, it is over. And now she is back at their bench. She sighs pleasurably and, looking up, sees him coming toward her. He is more bent than usual, and he leans more heavily on his cane. Then he pauses and lifts his head toward the bench. Making out a figure, he suddenly moves with new vigor, hardly touching his cane to the ground. He thinks I'm someone else and he's coming to evict me, Molly muses, grinning broadly. The fool! "So, look who it is!"

"Hello, Sam. How are you?"

"How should I be? I come every day. I sit. Your friends come looking for a handout. I tell 'em 'She's not here! Go away!' They look at me like it's my fault."

"You look fine, Sam."

"You look tired."

"I've been a little under the weather. I'm all right now. It's nothing. Really. Nothing."

"Nothing. When you don't know, nothing is something. Every day you come, then all of a sudden, you don't come. You couldn't tell me?"

"How could I tell you? I don't know how to reach you. And even if I did, I wouldn't want to worry you."

"So now from inside my head she talks. I could have maybe come to see you. Brought a bagel, whatever. Who knew what was happening?"

"Sam, you couldn't make the steps at my place. Next thing you know, you'd have a heart attack to bring me a bagel. Besides, Hannah knew. She called me almost every day."

"But she couldn't come, this fancy lawyer daughter of yours. Just like my Phil from Passaic. Too busy. Too important. All they know from is the telephone and the checkbook."

"I asked her not to come. My place is small. It's not good for company."

"Is that why you never cooked me a meal? I thought maybe you're afraid of me. For months, we sit on a bench in the park. We talk. Even the pigeons know from me. But you never say, 'Sam, come to my place. I'll make you a meal.' Then one day, you just stop coming. So I'm thinking, did I do something? Did I say something? Questions I have. What I don't have is answers."

"I'm not afraid of you, Sam. It's just . . . I don't . . . I don't eat fancy these days. My good things I gave to Hannah. Why, I haven't had company in so long I wouldn't know how to behave!"

"I'm not asking you to behave. To make a show. Just a meal. Maybe one day we could talk and it wouldn't be on a bench with pigeons squawking on my toes. If I had a kitchen, I would say, 'Molly, why don't you come to my place?' Nowadays, it's okay the man should invite. In my day, it was a different thing. But I don't have a kitchen. Only a burner."

"So that's why you eat so much at Katz's Cafeteria! I never realized."

"There's lotsa things we don't realize. Then something happens and we realize."

"I like coming to the park and visiting here. I'll tell you a secret. I like to pretend it's my own private garden. Like I lived on a big estate and entertained my guests here. Isn't that silly? Pretending like that at my age!"

"What's the difference — silly, not silly. At our age, you should be able to think whatever you want. Just like you should be able to talk and it shouldn't be always on a park bench."

"Oh, Sam! You're impossible!"

"I'm also hungry. So whadaya say we go to Katz's? You

look like you could use a good hot meal. Put some color in your cheeks. Come. I'll get the blintzes. You'll get the latkes, and we'll share."

"No, thanks, Sam. I'm not hungry. Maybe another time."

"What is it? She's glued to the bench? So I'll eat, and you'll have a chicken soup. If that's okay by you, Miss Stubborn."

"Okay, Sam. Okay. I'll have a cup of tea. Maybe a soup."

"Good. And maybe after I'll walk with you home so I'll see where you live. That way when you cook me a meal I'll know where to come so it shouldn't go to waste."

"And you call me stubborn?" she says, taking his arm to lift herself from the bench as he shoos away the pigeons with the tip of his cane.

"Who knows," he shrugs. "Sometimes, it pays off. One of these days I might even get a home-cooked meal."

"Who knows?" echoes Molly quietly, remembering with relief that she hasn't yet given Hannah her antique china tea set.

ELVIRA
✦ ✧ ✦
The Talking Vase

W ell, Lucille, you might just have waited a bit, don't
you think?" Elvira says, directing her comment to the
mantelpiece, which she will now have to rearrange.
"Incongruous. Utterly incongruous!"

She stares at the two vases, one tall and elegant, with
slender, hand-painted flowers growing up its body, the
other a squat of pottery with funky colors running into
each other haphazardly. Her exasperation is noticeable
in how she stands — erect and thrusting her petite bosom
out — and in the haughty tone of voice she always uses,
particularly with Lucille, whenever she is highly miffed. "I
mean, springing it on me like this! It's quite a shock, not
to say an inconvenience."

And isn't it just like Lucille, Elvira thinks, full of
impulse, always doing things on the spur. That was how
they'd met, nearly fifty-four years ago. They'd been working in the Women's League, in totally different parts of the
country, and would never have known a thing about each
other if it hadn't been for Lucille deciding at the very last
minute to come to the national convention, where they
met in the cafeteria line. "Mind if I join you?" Lucille had
said, sitting down before Elvira could even utter so much
as a "Please." And then had launched into how she came
to be active in the League and where she "spent energy," as
she liked to put it. Elvira, quieter and just finding her way
in marriage and young motherhood, had found her
enchanting, full of zest and sparkle. And, as it turned out,

they had a lot in common, besides the fact that they were both married to professional men and each had two young children. Both had come from immigrant families, had entertained ideas of travel and study when they were younger — thwarted, of course, by finances and expectations about "decent" women. In the end, they had skipped the conference's afternoon sessions and had gone instead to sit by the river where they talked until dinnertime, forging then and there the friendship that had sustained each of them through life's meandering and sometimes murky voyage.

And now Lucille had gone and ruined it all. Not that it wasn't inevitable, of course, nor that Elvira couldn't have been the one. It just seemed unfair after all the years of laughing about it, as if it would never happen, that it actually had.

It was only one of the things they laughed about over the years. "Do you remember," Elvira muses, forgetting her annoyance for the moment, "the time we went to Chicago, just the two of us? No husbands. No children. Just us, like schoolgirls, staying up all hours in the hotel room, ordering up room service and getting slightly tiddly on that rose wine! You did annoy me, never wanting to sleep, prancing around the room like Astor's pet pony set free. 'Elvira!' you said. 'Let yourself go! Enjoy it. You only live once!' You were always saying that, like it was your credo or something. I envied you it — that sprightly freedom that seemed a kind of trademark.

"And now look where we are. Not that it could be helped, really. One of us had to be the one. But you can't blame me for being annoyed. Leaving me to it like this. Always leaving me to it. 'You've got to get on with your life,' you said, when James left me and you stayed the two weeks that I nearly collapsed. 'I'm leaving you to it, Elvira, because I know you can do it.' Well, you were right, of course. You always did know me better than I knew myself. Still, it's a bit much."

Elvira moves closer to the fireplace and rests her fingers gently on the graceful vase. Like a blind person reading a poem in braille, she traces the china's patterns and designs with her fingertips, slowly and lovingly, so as not to miss any of their nuance. "When did we actually decide to do this?" she asks her friend, looking at the silver-framed picture of the two of them that had occupied the center of the mantelpiece for so very many years. "You know, we're just like these two vases," she says, distract-edly. "You're earthy, meant for living life's hard work. I'm so . . . fragile, in comparison. We even look like these silly things, me straight as a piece of bone china, and you sort of short and round. And now, you're here in your full-ness, and I'm feeling so empty . . . "

Sighing, Elvira picks up the china vase, holding its lid in place even though she knows it is sealed, and returns to her original question. "When did we decide to do this?" she murmurs, hugging the graceful vessel. And without a sound, the answer comes to her. "It was in Chicago, on that very trip, wasn't it, dear? When we were quite tiddly indeed, and you said, 'I know, Elvira! We could have a pact. Because we're best friends, and we really understand each other. Let's agree. Whoever dies first, the other gives the eulogy.' Then the next day, in Marshall Fields, you insisted suddenly on buying me this china vase. Just like that, on impulse, as we walked through the fine china department, you said, 'That's it! You must have that, so that when I die, you can keep my ashes! It's my gift to you, because you are my dearest friend!' you said, laughing yourself silly. The salesman was positively shocked. Didn't know what to make of it. I'd gotten used to you by then, of course. And then I decided that if I was to have your ashes, you should be prepared to receive mine. So when we passed that little pottery shop and you admired this funny old clay thing, which I must tell you, dear, I still find utterly unattractive, I bought it for you. And then we went back to the hotel and had champagne in the lobby bar. The whole thing was scandalous, really. But my, we had ourselves a time, didn't we? Dear, dear Lucille. How I shall miss you!

"Loren's note says you told him all about it, just before you lost consciousness. He never knew anything about it before then. No one did, he said. 'Funny,' he wrote, 'how children never really know certain things about their parents, who they are as people. My mother wanted you to have this. She made that quite clear. I assume the arrangement will meet with your approval, and I am grateful for your friendship to my mother. I look forward to seeing you at the memorial service, although I wish it could be under happier circumstances.' How cold and formal, so unlike you, Lucille.

"Now, how in the world shall we place these?" Elvira ponders, returning to the task at hand. "They're so . . . incongruous." Gently, she puts the china vase back on the mantel, at the far end of the pottery one, and steps back to assess the situation like a curator of great works of art. She frowns and rubs her finger across the creases in her top lip. "Oh, to hell with symmetry!" she says suddenly, and with one great, uncharacteristic, and determined motion, Elvira picks up the china vase and plunks it down right next to her own.

Then she takes up her gloves and purse, secures her hat with a pearl hat pin to her perfectly coiffured gray French twist, and sets off to deliver a eulogy that 'will knock their socks off,' as Lucille had put it, because that's what she promised her best friend one windy day in Chicago, when both of them were young and thought they would live forever.

✦ ◇ ✦
About the Author

Elayne Clift has been a professional writer and journalist for over ten years. She was the recipient in 1992 of the Award for Excellence in Journalism from the New Jersey Education Association. Her award-winning articles, essays, stories, poems, and travel writings have appeared in publications in North America, Europe, and Asia.

Her first book of essays, *Telling It Like It Is: Reflections of a Not So Radical Feminist,* was published in 1991. *The Road to Radicalism: Further Reflections of a Frustrated Feminist* appeared in 1994. *Demons Dancing in My Head,* a poetry collection, came out in 1995. Ms. Clift also compiled and edited an anthology entitled *But Do They Have Field Experience!* in 1993.

In addition to being a print journalist, Ms. Clift is Washington reporter for WINGS, an internationally syndicated radio program by and for women. She works as a consultant in international health and development communication and teaches at George Washington University, Yale University, and Emerson College. She holds a B.A. in English and an M.A. in communication, both from the University of Maryland.

Ms. Clift lives and crones in Potomac, Maryland. She and her husband have two grown children.

To order this or other titles by Elayne Clift, photocopy this coupon and send payment (check or money order) to:

OGN Publications

11320 Rouen Drive, Potomac, Maryland 20854
For customer service and other inquiries, call 1-800-622-5043

Please send me:

Qty	Title	Price ea.	Total
	Croning Tales	$12.95	
	Demons Dancing in My Head	$8.95	
	Telling It Like It Is	$14.95	
	The Road to Radicalism	$14.95	
		Subtotal	_____
	Shipping and Handling ($1/book)		_____
		Total	_____

Name _____

Address _____

City/State _____ Zip _____

Phone No. *(in case we have questions about your order)* _____